ILLUSION *of* MEMORY

ILLUSION *of* MEMORY

J. Z. Holden

CHOPIN PRESS
East Hampton, N.Y. 11937
2013

FIRST CHOPIN INTERNATIONAL EDITION, SEPTEMBER 2013

ISBN-10:1-4800-7537-X
ISBN-13: 978-1-4800-7537-5

Dedicated to Jules

We cannot regain what is lost, if only
because it never existed as we remember it.

—*Jonathan Boyarin*

ILLUSION *of* MEMORY

PART ONE

Jerusalem

Chapter 1

Diary Entry

Jerusalem
April 1, 1973

What could I have done differently? I blame myself, it's easier; that way, I live in the illusion that I had the power to correct whatever went wrong.

I do not believe in God, but this morning I prayed. Or more to the point, I tried to cut a deal. If only this time, God, please...let him come back. I promise I won't push him away again. The prayer is always followed by several demands: give me a sign; come on, prove that you exist by making him appear today, so that he can say he forgives me. Why should I believe in you if you don't give me a sign?

"Why do you always want to fight with me?" Amos says.

"I don't want to fight with you," I respond.

"Yes, you do. All the time. Your anger is unbearable."

My conversations with God are the same.

I fight with God. I fight with men. Can you imagine that?

Letter to Lizzie

Jerusalem
April 2, 1973

Dearest Lizzie in La-la Land,

Hello, my darling, how are you? I hope that Peter is treating you well? Mom and Dad have not written for months. It's been a year and a half and I still get lonely here. I wish you'd visit me before it's time to come home. Jerusalem is incredibly beautiful and there is so much to do. As you know, I live in a stunning old Arab house with lots of room. I've also joined a kibbutz, where I go on the weekends to visit my kibbutz family and artsy friends. Hurry, please. My show is slotted for October in New York and there isn't much time.

How are you spending your time in Los Angeles? What sorts of projects have you got under way? I haven't heard from you in a long time and am growing concerned. You know I miss you terribly when you are not around.

Want to hear about my life?

At this very moment, I am sipping a Pernod and water while sunning my legs at the artist café on Jerusalem's main drag. My former lover, Amos, the beautiful surrealist with the dark hair and blue eyes, is waving to me from his table. He is in the process of se-

4

ducing a tall, bony woman with chestnut hair and pale skin. She looks sixteen, but her body language says thirty. She is ethereal, perhaps she is a dancer. I have never seen her before. And I thought I'd seen everyone. She puffs on little black cigarillos without inhaling, in between sips of white wine. Watching them I feel jealous, but rather than make a scene, I lean back out of the sun.

As I settle in, he tilts his head and takes this woman's hand in his, then he slowly kisses the palm, never removing his gaze from her eyes.

He has ways of making you believe that your rejection is potentially fatal. I observe the wave of her pale, thin hand, and then, shaking a head of coppery curls, she looks away. He keeps on in his diligent and intense manner, cracking the occasional joke, banking on the amusing aside to disarm her, immediately prior to gently biting her palm.

This is the way his routine goes: he invites you to lunch at the café so that everyone can witness his most recent triumph, followed by the truck ride to the studio. He tells you to sit closer in the front seat of his old, sky-blue Ford pickup truck. Then he lights and passes you the enormous joint of hashish that he carefully rolled earlier that morning. The joint gets passed back and forth several times. At this point, he usually initiates some meaningful looks, delicate touching, and then more jokes. You're both stoned and hot for each other and the heat from the desert makes you want to take off your clothes and do it right there in the car. That is, of course, just the way he wants it. As if to prolong your desire, he makes one last stop: the ragged edge of the overlook from which he threatens, in jest, to throw you. And because you are so stoned that you can barely stand up, you laugh uncontrollably as if this is the funniest thing you've ever heard in your life. In hindsight, many have wished he'd thrown them off as an act of kindness.

The Middle East is a place of the senses. And I am learning that not unlike parts of Europe, love and seduction are a national pastime. Israelis appear to be flexible people, and monogamy, although admired, is not considered a cultural necessity. I wonder whether the national appreciation for sexual variety is a counterbalance to the stress of endless war?

Perhaps knowing that death is always uncomfortably near, and assuming the opportunity presents itself (and it always seems to, doesn't it?), making love is life affirming. Of course, the French have no such excuse, and yet insist on cinq a sept with the same fervor with which they insist on the correct wine. Alors everywhere, even in America, consensual sexual variety has become a way of life. I am ambivalent.

I can't truly love someone and actually take joy in him doing with anyone the intimate things he does with me. And so, Amos and I have reached an impasse.

I need a monogamous, committed relationship in order to feel sexually free, and he can't bear not being totally open.

I'm very sad and lonely without him, but trying not to let it show.

So, write soon.

Much love,
Ta Bête
La Bette

Chapter 2

Diary Entry

Jerusalem
April 3, 1973

I now realize that my obsession with transvestite prostitutes began with a conversation I happened to overhear as a child. It was raining and cold, sometime in autumn or early winter, and the women were making hot coffee and taking Hungarian pastries out of boxes labeled Rigo.

Accompanying the clatter of plates and forks, there was the symphony of burps made by the coffeemaker. Beneath the din, I could hear them arguing in German about whether or not the camps had had brothels.

My grandmother, who seemed the most knowledgeable of the three, giggled as she reminded them that her sister and her sister's daughter, their aunt Rosa and cousin Litta, respectively, had survived the war by operating a bordello. The women laughed, and covered their mouths in shame, and then uttered the words, *"Pssttt! Neske kiteire!"* A phrase spoken in the Yiddish klezmer language that meant stop talking, the kid's within hearing distance.

As I grew older, I learned that camp prostitutes,

both female and male, were kept in a special district where for a little extra bread and some vodka, they were encouraged to wear departed Jewish women's furs and black lace garters, leather high-heeled boots, feather boas and strings of pearls.

Caught between revulsion and wonder, I tried to envision whether a Nazi who had seen too much might actually find solace in the image of a boy in women's clothes. More than likely, the sexual act, in whatever form it took, must have been a momentary escape into a private, fetishistic flight of the imagination, a domination fantasy reinforcing all the other unspeakable acts.

My favorite sexual fantasy of the moment is to be a priestess who resides in a Greek temple. I choose my lovers from among the temple's followers. And in exchange for what is seen as their direct hotline to the Divine, I am presented with luxurious material sacrifices.

Priestesses were, after all, the only women in Greek culture to be truly free because they were not owned and concealed by their husbands. They lived openly in society, doing as they pleased while being worshipped; something I would find most desirable. As the embodiment of divine power, priestesses are enviable creatures. Free to engage in whatever sex pleases them, their liberated sexuality serves a higher purpose.

Seeing that Greek men thought true love was possible only with other men, they sought out young boys, at times dressing them as women, leaving the strong and independent women the option of living a rich spiritual and sexual life; a solution some say was truly made in heaven.

Twice weekly, I travel to Tel Aviv where I watch the transvestite prostitutes parade down Hayarkon Street. They remind me of fallen stars in a Fellini movie. Quite ordinary men stop their cars for them, everyday folks who work in offices and then go home to their wives and children, just regular guys who have somehow developed a taste for something that looks like a poor man's Monica Vitti or Anita Ekberg.

One morning, a fistfight broke out between a transvestite and a female prostitute in bright daylight while people were driving to work. The female was loudly accusing the transvestite of taking over her turf and taking away her business. The transvestite shot back that if she had been doing a good job of it she never would have lost her clients to him in the first place. It was eight o'clock in the morning and they were both in full makeup, wearing garish clothes, fishnet stockings, and platform shoes. When words slipped into rolling punches on the ground, they became a mass of arms and legs, long fingernails, and false eyelashes squirming on the sidewalk. The female suddenly made a grab for the transvestite's wig, pulling it off, exposing his short black hair. Holding the wig pressed firmly between her breasts, she ran up the street laughing at the top of her lungs. The transvestite fell to his knees on the sidewalk and cried.

Meanwhile, all the neighbors who had come out to watch stood around telling him what to do.

"Don't take that bullshit from her! It's your street, too!"

Another neighbor chimed in. "Who does she think she is, anyway?"

An older, unkempt woman with wild, thick gray hair wearing a greasy housedress and a stained apron, with yellow plastic flip-flops on her gnarled feet, walked through the crowd and, placing her meaty arms around him, kissed the top of his head, helped him up, and invited him in for a cup of tea.

Ironically, the dreams began the very next night. For months, I've awakened to a sweat-drenched body choking in damp sheets. Sometimes I awake several times a night. I dream that I am pursued, but cannot scream. Finally, and with the utmost effort, I manage a puny, "Help me!" The sound of my own voice wakes me, and my legs, which are tangled in the clammy sheets, abort my attempts to run. In the background, I hear John Philip Sousa conducting a band playing *"America the Beautiful."* After a few moments, I realize that it is a dream. I settle down and close my eyes. It is then that a persistent thought presents itself, one that has followed me for years, like a stray dog looking for a meal.

The voice says,

"The enemy is not on the outside."

Damn, if it wasn't another one of life's fucking riddles.

Illusion of Memory

Chapter 3

Letter to Bette
The Grand Hotel du Mal
Northern California
April 10, 1973

My dearest, dearest Monkey-Head (I can call you that because I'm your older sister),

I'm on vacation and thought I'd write a few words to my babysistertheadventuress. Did you know that life is a quest? By now, Mom and Dad have probably told you that Peter and I have separated. I've been seeing a shrink to help me get over it. And I've started writing in addition to painting—isn't that amazing?—so it must be working.

I used to see him twice weekly on Tuesdays and Thursdays, at precisely 4:15 p.m. I'd be early for our appointments, even though I seemed to be late for almost everything else. From my seat by the door, I would hear muffled men's voices through his walls. I wondered what other people talked to him about. The last time I was there, as I sat waiting my turn, the door to his office opened and out walked the well-dressed guy who never makes eye contact. Instead, he clutches his soft leather, one-thousand-dollar briefcase tightly to his chest while following the invisible line on the floor that leads to the exit. I think he's crazy, but then again, if I'm there, I must be too, eh?

Dr. Prince always holds the door to his office open, beckoning me to enter.

"Hi. C'mon in," he says.

His real name is Dr. Prince, and I feel like Cinderella stepping into his magic realm. During our first session he asked me to share my earliest recollections.

When I explained that they occurred when I was twelve, he told me that I had unceremoniously albeit unconsciously deleted a sizable chunk of my memory, since no matter how hard I tried, no earlier recollections were forthcoming.

Because he considers himself a master technician, the good doctor believes he has what it takes to retrieve the first twelve years from wherever I've hidden them. Isn't that weird?

The way he sees it, therapy is something called a mind program, something that can be altered. All I need to do is absorb it and then I'll be a living miracle.

I take medicine, too, something called LSD. He supervises me. It's a little like truth serum and it makes me hallucinate. Other doctors, like Timothy Leary, have been taking it and say that it opens up all sorts of pathways to consciousness and understanding.

So far, I've been a lump of sugar in a sugar bowl and I've heard music bounce off the walls of the bowl!

Last week I saw the teeny shells in the sidewalk grow. After the trips are over, I have really amazingly colorful dreams.

The Prince, as I like to call him, knows that I really don't believe in therapy. He knows that I am an expressionist painter, and that I'm afraid if we get to the root of my depression I will lose my creativity. So I take great pleasure in giving him a difficult time precisely because he is so darn hell-bent on changing me and I do not, as the joke goes, really want to change. You know me; I want the world to change.

"So, how are you?" he queries.

Of course, when he says it, it means something vastly different from when you ask or even Peter says it. He wants to know how my internal life is doing.

Isn't that cool?

"Well, just yesterday as I was swimming laps," I said last time, "I had the strangest sensation. It was as if I had remembered a piece of film, a scene from my life that had been cut at an editing session and was lying on the floor. In the tranquility of the water, when I saw it in my mind's eye, it felt like a shard of glass cutting my brain."

I liked that last touch. It was symbolic of my pain.

"Go on," said the Prince.

"I'm riding in the backseat of a white Impala convertible with red interior, and the roof is down. My aunt is driving and my mother is sitting next to her.

We're on our way to Jones Beach. I'm about three, maybe four years old. The radio is blaring and we're singing, *'Que sera, sera, whatever will be, will be, the future's not ours to see, que sera, sera'...that's it."* (You weren't born yet...)

Since I know that the Prince plays the drums, I assumed he had inherently good timing. But, I was wrong.

"Well, what do you think?" he asked.

"There's also a dream," I interjected, with a riff of my own, "that I had last night."

"Go on," he said.

This was the most excited he'd ever been. Maybe he'd slept well the night before and wouldn't doze off. I'd noticed that every once in a while his eyelids would close and his breathing would get very steady. I know that he sleeps. I just keep talking till he wakes up. How I've ended up in therapy, paying a total stranger to listen to what is on my mind, is beyond me. But get ready for this:

The dream takes place in a mental institution that's like a tower of Babel for women. No two people speak the same language. You can't really tell the patients from the doctors; everybody wears these gauzy white robes that make us look like angels, and we all float around like we're in heaven, but nobody really understands anything that anybody else says.

I'm hanging out, just doing my usual float from

place to place, when I become very tired and fall asleep on the first available operating table that happens to be standing in the corner of the room. I wake up because I can't breathe. I realize that my mother, grandmother, and aunt are all lying on top of me, smothering me. Then I feel hands and fingers hiking up my nightgown. And suddenly someone is fondling my genitals, but I can't tell who.

The dream woke me up. I was so freaked out that I never got back to sleep.

Pretty wild, huh?

Dr. Prince is a Jewish American Prince, and for reasons he's refused to discuss, he has chosen the children of Holocaust survivors as the focus of his practice. I don't get what the fuss is about, but we qualify. I told him that all the family except for you, Mom and Dad, Mom's sister, and Grandma went up in smoke. He finds it odd that their demise was never discussed.

Do you remember all those Eastern European intellectuals, all the artists and musicians who came to the house when we were little? They'd play the piano and sing in foreign languages, and after a couple of drinks they'd speak in English with heavy accents, and we'd all dance? That was really all there was to it, wasn't it?

For some reason, Dr. Prince has other ideas. He's a pain in the ass sometimes, but I like him because he is willing to argue with me even though he stutters.

I've noticed that when he gets passionate about a point he's making, his stutter disappears.

We sat around in silence for a long time. He still wasn't saying anything about the dream. I couldn't tell whether he was thinking about the content when he looked up at the ceiling, or whether he was suppressing a fart. All that was clear was that he needed additional time.

Eventually, he pushed his glasses up with the tip of his right index finger, pulled several tissues out of the box beside him and blew his nose, removing several big boogers that had been bothering him, and said, "Do you really want to know what I think?"

"Not really," I said.

He leaned forward in his leather therapist's chair and looked me in the eye. Then he whispered, "I think you were sexually abused by your mother."

"Would you speak up?" I said. "You won't believe what I thought you said. I thought you said I was abused by my mother. That's a riot. What would you call that, a Freudian hearing slip?"

"That is what I said."

"That's ridiculous," I said.

"The dream tells me you were sexually abused by your mother."

"The dream tells me it was all three of them."

"I'm serious."

"Are you saying I can't remember because something happened?"

"More than something."

I picked an imaginary piece of lint off my slacks and wondered whether I should leave.

"This is completely unacceptable."

"Why?" the Prince asked.

"They're Holocaust survivors."

"Precisely, you've been gas lit."

"This is no time to be making puns and talking about a movie starring Ingrid Bergman."

"All right, I'll behave. But do you understand what I mean?"

"Do people come in here and tell you stuff like this all day long?"

"Unfortunately, they do."

"How do you take it, day after day?"

"I think most people are despicable."

"Despondent."

"Stop correcting me."

"I know you didn't mean what you said about my mother."

"We're running out of time," he said, and pointed to his wristwatch.

"Figuratively or literally? How am I going to get well if at the most horrifyingly critical moment in my life I run out of time?"

"Because now, the memories should start."

"Oh, great. What's that going to be like? 'We interrupt regular broadcasting to bring you this special bulletin?'"

"Probably."

"Stop it, you're scaring me."

"When the person you are supposed to be able to trust most betrays you, that sets up a pattern for life."

"I've read the book, thanks. And while we're on the subject, that's persons, plural."

"You've got to go now. I'll see you on Thursday."

"I'm not leaving," I said.

"You have my number if you need to talk. I'm sorry, my next patient is waiting."

Can you believe him? The nerve! So I said, "You can't just pry me open like a thousand-year-old mollusk and hang me out to dry. I'm not who I thought I was. They're not who I thought they were. My entire life is a pack of lies, and I'm not going to take it anymore!"

"*Network*, by Sidney Lumet at his fabulous best! Look, it's understandable that you're angry. You might consider renting *Twelve Angry Men*."

"Will you cut that out?" I said.

"I'm sorry. I'll give you fifteen minutes."

"You and Andy Warhol."

I stood up and headed for the door. I wasn't going to take that!

"I'm not going to take your rejection personally," he said. "I'll see you on Thursday."

"I suggest that between now and then you hold your breath," I said and slammed the door behind me.

The gall of that man.

When I stepped into the street, it was dark and felt like snow. People were rushing home from work. I was in shock. I stepped into the flow of human bodies.

The next thing I knew, I was standing in front of our apartment door. From the hallway, I could hear the clatter of pots and pans. When I entered, I smelled the welcoming aroma of stew simmering and was touched that Peter would prepare dinner without my asking.

"Hi. I'm home," I shouted.

"Perfect timing. Dinner's almost done," he yelled from the kitchen.

I couldn't wait to hug him. When I walked into the kitchen, he was standing at the stove wearing my favorite navy blue cashmere dress.

"What's going on?" I asked.

"What do you think?" he said, turning toward me, ladle in hand.

"Why are you wearing my dress?"

"I like cashmere."

"This is an unprecedented event."

"I was going to wait until dessert to tell you, but I might as well tell you now. I've made an appointment to have a sex change operation."

"Just like that? You've decided to cut off my favorite part of your anatomy? Can't we talk about this?"

"Nope, my mind's made up."

I can't remember what happened next. All I know is that I woke up in the most glorious mansion in the country surrounded by green rolling hills. Even more surprising, I discovered I was wrapped up like a Christo. At my unraveling, which was a spectacular not-to-be-missed event, where everyone who was anyone was present, they awarded me my own magnificent room, and the first thing I did was paint it Chinese lacquer red. It's so vital against the stark white of all the walls, floor, and furniture.

This week I started preparing my new exhibition. I'm working on a series of red-on-red paintings as an Ode to Rothko. All the staff here is exceptionally kind and very supportive. They are more than happy to share their drugs with me and now I'm in high spirits all the time.

Knowing my passion for color, the chef orders every imaginable kind of edible flower. Unfortunately, the nasty hoteliers have drawn the line at my redesigning the staff uniforms to match my paintings, which was quite upsetting. But the maids, being sympathetic to my cause, opened a bottle of Veuve Clicquot and shared more of their fabulous designer drugs, so now I don't really give a shit what color they wear.

I'm just having the best time. The most fascinating guests are vacationing here. There's a poet, several very well-known writers, and a sculptor who makes enormous bronzes that look like dog poop. And just this morning, the hosts, who are definitely not rocket scientists, informed me that it will be spring soon, as if I couldn't figure that out for myself. The best news of all is that when the weather breaks, my Prince has promised to take me with him on his daily rides in his white convertible. I don't know which I'm more excited about, riding through the countryside with the top down or watching the vintage movies in his private film library.

I know you're having an incredible time screwing all those gorgeous Israelis, so please write soon, and send some slides of your transvestite paintings. I think the crowd up here would be extremely appreciative. When are you planning on coming home? Or are you?

Don't worry about me, I'm having the time of my life. And as for that dream interpretation, the Prince has taken it all back. By the way, I have a fabulous new address: Moi, c/o The Grand Hotel du Mal somewhere in the hills outside San Francisco.

Love, love, love,
Your Lizzie in a Tizzy

Illusion of Memory

Journal Entry

Jerusalem
April 20, 1973

I have received the most disturbing letter from
Lizzie. They've put her in a nuthouse somewhere in
Northern California. However, she thinks she's in a
love hotel surrounded by fantastically creative and entertaining guests. Peter leaving her to have a sex
change operation is unbelievable.   ·

She told me that he's fallen in love with an English-
man. They plan to move to London after his surgery
and as soon as the divorce is final. I am beside myself.
It's all so terribly, terribly sad and frightening. I am wor-
ried sick about her. She has always coped with difficulties by denying their existence and escaping into an
imaginary world. It is part of what makes her such a remarkable artist and creative spirit. But her denial has
never gone this far before. On the other hand, she
does not sound as if she is suffering. Perhaps it is I,
who believe myself to be grounded in reality with eyes
and heart open, who is actually the crazy one? Who is to
say? And besides, if my parents have had her committed, there may be nothing I can do.

I know I'm being selfish, but oh how thankful I am
that I live in such a spiritual and peaceful place so far
away from them, with thousands of miles between us

to protect me from the constant turmoil. Israel is experiencing such peace and prosperity. I feel utterly safe here. I can leave my doors unlocked at night, can walk down the street alone regardless of the time. Even if I were drunk as hell, I'd never have to worry that someone would try to harm me. On the contrary, people are helpful, kind, and generous, and most of them have so little. I suppose Israelis are happy to be alive. Tel Aviv is open twenty-four hours a day; the restaurants, bars, and cafés beckon, and the men! Oh, the men in their uniforms are so beautiful.

Meanwhile, in my little world, it will reach ninety degrees today. I am living languorous moments, painting, taking photographs, and studying Jewish mysticism at Hebrew University. The classroom where the Kabbalah class is held overlooks Mount Scopus. Each week I sit by the window that has an unobstructed view of the holiest shrines in civilization. From my seat by the casement I can see the narrow, ancient cobblestone walkway, the Via Dolorosa, the road Jesus walked as he bore the cross to his death. At the bottom lies the Church of the Holy Sepulcher where his body was later laid to rest. The Western Wall, the only surviving part of the Great Temple of Jerusalem that was not destroyed by the Romans, stands ravaged in Jerusalem's ruthless light. The temple was certainly Judaism's last vestige of greatness. What seems like only a few feet away is the Dome of the Rock, built on the sacred ground where Abraham prepared to surrender his son to God, and where Muhammad ascended to heaven.

Each week, I observe these holy places teeming with activity, quietly coexisting side by side as the Kabbalah teacher, an American living and teaching in Israel, explains the significance of the Tree of Life and its many complex branches divided down the middle by the feminine on one side, and the masculine on the other. For a few moments at least, the mysteries of life are defined. Given that anything can be illuminated, even the unfathomable, Kabbalists believe that multiple realities live side by side. It is therefore paramount to ask the correct questions. When the correct words are found to form the argument, the mystery may be penetrated. If a certainty, a cornerstone exists, it is that nothing is as it seems. If something turns out to be as it appears, then that thing, that person, that situation is considered closest to God. The language of mysticism is poetic, erotic in its passion, in its longing to merge with an unseen world.

The mystical lessons fly, one into the other, as the day itself sinks into the surrounding hills like a sidewinder burying itself in the desert sand. I often wonder why we in the modern world no longer see one another ascend to heaven. I've concluded those old religious guys had style. How many people can even take to the air in their dreams? Isn't it Erica Jong who just recently made us aware that as a culture we have a fear of flying?

My favorite day of the week is the Sabbath. I particularly enjoy walking down the old secluded streets of Rehavia, one of the two areas where the Hasidim live and where driving cars from Friday evening through Saturday at sundown is forbidden. I linger in the hope of catching snippets of conversation in Yiddish.

One evening, two scholars aged seven and nine, respectively, walked in front of me twirling payes between small fingertips. They were utterly oblivious to my presence while I hung on their every word. Can you imagine, they were interpreting and arguing a passage from the Talmud?

Frail, small, and bespectacled, wearing knickers rather than long pants, with white stockings and buckled shoes that clicked on the stones as they walked, the assertions of the nine-year-old were astute! As if he were inhabited by the soul of an aged and wise scholar who offered intellectual advice incisive beyond his years. The younger boy argued brilliantly and made his point directly, as the older one listened quietly and considered.

All the while, they were walking in the direction of the local schul where their fathers and older brothers were praying. The ecstatic intimacy with the soul that they possessed was unspeakably beautiful. And perhaps secretly I hoped that by getting close enough, their gift for intellectual discourse in the realm of the spiritual would rub off on me.

My parents have never asked me how I spend my time. I would like to share how much I love my life here. But whenever I attempt to tell them, they change the subject to interfamily politics. Mom has stopped talking to Grandma and Grandma is no longer seeing Aunt Sylvia. When I ask Mom why there is so much turmoil in our family, her response is always the same: certain things are simply not forgivable.

Illusion of Memory

Chapter 4

Letter to Lizzie

Jerusalem
April 21, 1973

Dearest Lizzie,

I am so sorry about you and Peter. And I'm taking great pleasure in saying I told you so. In addition, you are trying to convince me that you're in an artists' hotel on a glorious lake, but I've got the most horrendous feeling that you're not staying in a hotel, baby cakes. I know you're going to want to know how I've reached this conclusion, older and wiser sister, so sit down please.

When I try to phone you, I get a Nurse Rat-a-tansky on the line, and believe me or not, she won't let me talk to you. You're either in session with your shrink, or in solitary for not having eaten your dinner the night before, or having a nervous breakdown in your group therapy session. If that's a hotel, I'm living at the palace with the queen of England. What the hell is going on, and are you OK? Did Mom and Dad sign you away to some high-class nuthouse, or do you still have some say about things?

Call me, Lizzie, since I can't reach you. I don't

know whether she's told you, but Mom is going into the hospital today. They've found a lump.

They say it's all very "routine." She's gone off the deep end; she calls me crying all day long. Each time she phones, she asks me, "Why me? Why me? What did I do to deserve this?"

I don't know what to say or what to do and I wish you were here. I miss you and need you terribly.

> Love,
> Ta Bête XOXOXOXOXOXO
> Bette

Letter to Bette
The Grand Hotel du Mal

Northern California
May 3, 1973

My dearest Monkey-Head,

I'm so glad to receive your letter, but so utterly shocked by its content. Of course I'm living in a hotel, you silly little thing. There's absolutely nothing to be afraid of, and if you are getting someone called Nurse Rat-a-tan-sky on the telephone, you must be dialing the wrong number. Usually Eduardo, the concierge, takes all our calls, and you'd know his voice because he's the most charming Italian from Venice, and speaks English with the most divine accent.

How terrible that you're in Israel, darling, but you know, we shy away from newspapers here, they do nothing for our creativity or our well-being. On the contrary, the news is so utterly depressing and hopeless that most of us get into a bit of a snit after reading the paper or watching TV. So we don't. I was never a big current events person, anyway, as you know.

I am amazed that you remember things about our growing up at all. I don't remember a thing prior to the age of twelve. Did I mention that? Well, I don't. There doesn't seem to be any purpose. But now that I think of it, I recall Mom and Dad having a huge falling-out when I was fifteen. Didn't they separate for a time? When they decided to give things another try, we moved to the city and attended that school where we had to wear those awful gray pleated skirts and navy blazers. You see, I remember a great deal.

You were busy taking ballet classes and piano lessons after school. Dad worked all the time, even pulling all-nighters and sleeping over at the office.

I try not to think of the past. It's as if nothing existed prior to our lives on East 74th Street.

And of course, four years later I was married to Peter and traveling all over the world. Who would have thought he'd turn out to be gay?

Tell me more about your transvestite paintings, Monkey-Head. The subject matter is so totally taboo, it's marvelous. You must be kinkier than I ever imagined. You might consider calling Peter—he's planning on having a sex change soon. You could paint him if you like, or photograph him at the very least.

Imagine how sensational it would be to photograph him before and after!

What was the surrealist like in bed? We never compare notes anymore now that we're grown. I still remember dating a German in high school twice who was intense in all the right ways. Wish I had married him instead, come to think of it.

There's something extraordinary happening here at the hotel. It's such a very spiritual and loving place. Twice a week, at cocktails we drink champagne laced with LSD, and then for the next twenty-four hours or so we're off tripping the light fantastic. I can't begin to describe the insights I've had. For example, the separation we perceive between one another, our environment, even air and space and matter, does not exist. The separation is an illusion. When I squint, I see that everything is energy in different forms.

I've also seen God on a number of occasions and we've had the most interesting talks. He thinks you're a really talented artist, and finds your fascination with integrating the sexual elevated in the extreme.

He says you have superior intelligence and he's keeping a close eye on you, to make sure you keep going in the right direction. He hasn't contacted you because he says you're not quite ready yet, but it will be soon, and you don't have to worry about going out to find him, because he'll find you! He's everywhere!

And then there's that matter of unconditional love. We didn't get a lot of that at home when we were growing up. But here at the (dare I say it?) Love Hotel—there I've said it, coined it—it permeates everything. We're steeped in love. And so there's no fear here, nothing and no one to fear. Just love. Why don't you come up for a weekend or two? I know you are busy working on that series of paintings, but try to take some time for yourself. Besides, I miss you and would love to see you.

I'll phone you this week. Clear your schedule.

Love,
Lizzie the Lover

P.S. Don't worry about Mom. She'll be fine. And no matter what you do, don't indulge her!

Chapter 5

Diary Entry

Jerusalem
May 6, 1973

The Arab house in which I live sits at the top of a grassy hill, slouched in the shade of several craggy, aging cypress trees. The stone building is believed to be over two hundred years old. A gravely, earthen road leads up the steep embankment to the front door, first weaving through an orchard fragrant with apricot trees, then fusing as if by magic with another trail that twists through an olive grove, lush with bright new olives.

This ancient corridor has always felt strangely familiar to me, as it meanders toward a lavishly carved, though slightly rusted, metal door, which the Moroccan landlady has painted a bright turquoise-blue, to protect the inhabitants from the evil eye.

The house has a private interior foyer, dark and cool. With shades drawn, bright slats of light spill onto primeval black, white, and gray geometric tiles that cascade across the floor like an Escher drawing. Delicate lavender morning mists, followed by blazing midday heat storms, melt into sumptuous, fiery sunsets, descending inescapably into barely audible twinkling lights nestled in fallen pine needles, like Bedouin women wrapped in their diellabas, smelling of saffron, nutmeg, and honey, coupled with ripening fruit.

Each afternoon at five o'clock, the neighbor's schizophrenic daughter returns from her special school and the pitch-black cat, Ziggy Stardust, who is afraid of her, escapes to my studio where, purring contentedly, he sits resolutely Sphinx-like, while I paint in the room with the perfunctorily diffused northern light. Feet tucked beneath him, Ziggy purrs loud as a Harley, the sound filling my consciousness like background music, until I throw my brushes into the Savarin can filled with turpentine, shout "Fuck all!" at the top of my lungs, light a cigarette, remove my paint-splattered shoes, and walk out into the garden in my bare feet, signaling that work is done for the day.

The cat eventually rises, his back arching. Then, with paws stretched out in front of him, he elongates to twice his normal size like a piece of taffy. When he is ready, he will walk toward me, rubbing against my legs, nuzzling me in the direction of the kitchen, where he knows that his patience will be rewarded by an offering of cold milk.

I am preparing an exhibition of paintings to complete my master's degree. They will be shown at a gallery in New York City. I have sent a letter to the gallery requesting an extension by claiming to be behind schedule. They haven't yet responded, so I am assuming they are in agreement. The thought of returning to my old apartment in Brooklyn, the sound of the el clattering day and night, echoing the utter heartlessness and desolation of the city, is making me feel nothing short of despondent.

To comfort myself, I take another look around as a reminder that I really am in Jerusalem, standing in the garden next to my studio, my sanctuary. The room is a perfect square, twenty by twenty feet with two large windows of old French glass that are so wavy that when you look through them the hill across the way seems to be under water.

Even on sunny days, the northern light is cool, the air dry and clear.

Below and to the left of the olive grove is a group of darkish pines reflected in an artificial sweet water pond. As I work in the studio in the early mornings, my heart softens to the sound of hundreds of little birds that visit each day. In between each stroke of charcoal against paper or canvas, I hear them, playfully pursuing one another as they brush against the leaves of grass.

The studio walls are made of stone, covered in thick white plaster the consistency of stucco. Pressed into them like a mosaic are shiny metal thumbtacks holding up hundreds of black-and-white contact sheets. Alongside them, haphazardly overlapping one another, are sketches, small oil paintings, and magazine cutouts held together with white masking tape. The wall resembles a crowded collage composed of thousands of images of transvestites.

The bathroom transforms into a temporary lab where the images are developed and printed on polycontrast paper. Then they are hung alongside the window to dry, like eight-by-ten pieces of wet laundry flapping in the breeze. Some of the "girls" pose in various stages of undress, while others have chosen to be memorialized in full drag.

My compulsion to observe them is overwhelming. Some force has taken hold of my subconscious, and the two are dancing a deranged tango. In the quieter moments, when the background music lessens, I can overhear them chatting, as if cocktails were being served on the veranda. And when they have had one too many, loud arguments develop between the many memories that aren't even mine.

In my bedroom, there is a crack that runs across the ceiling like a border between countries. There was never a question in my mind that it was one ceiling. The crack might move, could head in another direction, the ceiling could fall apart and be rebuilt. Often I ask out loud, "If this ceiling fell apart, would people fight over who owned it? And if so, how many years would the War of the Ceilings last? How many casualties would there be? And who would pay reparations? Was there a point? Had I come into this life to fight over a piece of ceiling and then die?"

For years, I recognized the voices of the many arguments in my head as members of the Committee. Arguing with the Committee has always been exhausting. The only thing that seems to quell their passion is chocolate. Therefore, after a chocolate-eating episode one afternoon, I began to question whether God might perhaps live in Switzerland.

Gustav, our father's uncle who lived in Switzerland, was married to a German opera singer. When the war broke out, they remained together at his wife's insistence, and in order to fuel her sense of political outrage they decided to live in Bern. She had never asked him to convert, but one day he simply did.

Not that it would have mattered.

The reason for the conversion, he claimed, was that Christ appeared to him as he awoke from an afternoon nap. His daughter, Helga, confirmed that she was the first to find out, since it had been her job to wake him, lest he oversleep and miss his evening performance.

Afterward, everyone in the family attempted to question him, but he categorically refused to discuss what Christ had said. All anyone knew was that each day from that day forward, a man who had previously chased anything in a skirt at every available opportunity now still did so, but afterward went to church, prayed, and during the service ate a great deal of chocolate.

I took Gustav's religious experience to mean that he had established a family tradition: God would choose an odd moment to speak to us all. Knowing this, I was merely waiting for my moment to arrive. And by being in Jerusalem, I had hoped that God would choose to speak to me here—and sooner rather than later.

Perhaps I had been wrong. Possibly I would have to go to Switzerland to meet God. Conceivably, there in the pristine air of Goldiwil, ten thousand feet above sea level, listening to the mooing of cows and the clanging of bells, after devouring one too many dark chocolate Easter eggs, maybe Jesus would appear. And perhaps he would tell me what he'd said to Gustav. And perhaps he would transmit to me, for the first time in my short life, his secret elixir for peace that seems to so elude us all.

This morning, during an uncharacteristic respite from my usual self-absorbed self-immolation, I became aware of a bizarre paradox. On the one hand, we Jews had ultimately responded to the Nazi persecution and the world's reluctant aid by saying,

"Hitler, boy, you got us so wrong. We're the best! And we're gonna kick your ass!"

Unfortunately, we did so a bit too late, and at precisely the same moment that we internalized the unerring belief that blond was better, was stronger, was more attractive. As a blond you could be a mole in the other world. You could be mistaken for a Nazi or an American.

A blond preference seems to have existed since the Romans. Their transvestites and prostitutes used German hair color in bars of soap.

There, you see; "bars of soap" is a simple, meaningless phrase. But, whenever I hear the phrase "bars of soap" I think of the gas chambers. It's pathetic, really.

But I do digress. Apparently, blond has always communicated status; has always communicated Aryan, strength, and coolness; has even, as in the case of Marilyn, communicated the promise of extraordinary sexuality. Blond has for centuries bespoken allure.

After decade upon decade of abuse infused with the occasional assimilation fantasy, I couldn't help but wonder: what else had we managed to internalize? There was never really any getting away from it.

Even Ralph Lauren, *née Lifschitz*, would sell us the dream of belonging, at retail.

But I am getting ahead of myself. Despite my blondness and its accompanying allure, a particular brand of Holocaust Judaism pursues me—while in the shower, while painting, while photographing, and while speaking to Lizzie in Los Angeles. What is it I am trying so desperately to forget?

Illusion of Memory

Chapter 6

Jerusalem
May 7, 1973

Because I have fair skin, blonde hair, and blue eyes, Israelis assume I am German or Swedish or Dutch. They also assume that I am Christian.

When I explain that our family is of German and Polish descent and that I am Jewish, they reply without a hint of cynicism that I don't look Jewish.

I had a rather remarkable and apropos conversation today with Amos. He believes that he is above conditioning, that he has a totally open mind. After we made love (I know I shouldn't have, but I couldn't help myself; I hadn't seen him since we broke up), I sensed he might go all mushy on me, but instead, he surprised me and said, "So, your grandparents were murdered at Treblinka?"

I was taken aback.

"In the first transport from the Warsaw Ghetto," I responded. "And yours?"

"Auschwitz."

He got out of bed, stepped into his Levi's and zipped his fly. He grabbed his pack of cigarettes with one hand and shook them upward, allowing a single cigarette to pop up. Seizing it between his teeth, he threw the rest of the pack down on the table, then he flipped open a Zippo lighter. It sounded like flint against stone; the smell of lighter fluid permeated the air and a flame shot out of his cupped hands. Then he inhaled deeply on the Marlboro (Israeli cigarettes would never do) and, snapping the lighter shut, he tossed the Zippo a bit too roughly onto his desk littered with drawings. We spend the next five minutes in silence. He continued smoking and staring at me lying naked on the bed. Finally, he looked away and reached for the denim shirt hanging on the back of the chair.

Then he said, "Do your parents ever talk about it?"

I watched the smoke billow from his nostrils, and I imagined the smoke of burning bodies rising out of the chimneys of the crematoria.

"What is there to talk about?" I say. "Yours?"

"They were the first to settle a kibbutz in the Negev desert in 1948, long before that beautiful pipeline was built that brings all the water." He smiled a smile that said they were his heroes.

"My parents were in the underground," I say.

"Were they ever caught?"

"Thrown into prison," I say.

I thought to myself, WASPs discuss which Ivy League schools their parents attended, while children of the Holocaust discuss which camps their parents survived.

"How come you don't look Jewish?"

Suddenly he looked at me as if I might be lying to him, as if I was concealing the real story, that I was a German pretending to be Jewish. I felt him trace the lines of my body with his eyes. Despite my discomfort I didn't cover myself with the sheet. If this was some kind of test, I could handle it. I could see a thought pass through his brain as his gaze soften. Maybe he was thinking that my mother had been raped by a Nazi and that my life, having been tinged by tragedy in that way, made my looks forgivable.

"Our father likes to blame it on the Cossacks," I say.

Then, as I turned on my side, I smiled to let him know I wasn't serious. I knew that the Surrealist liked the explanation because he laughed. Finally I sensed, for this moment I was accepted.

Jews have a concentration camp hierarchy. The more severe the camp's reputation, the greater the "ah" of recognition that implies respect. Every child of a survivor knows that no matter how brave we are in the present, no matter how extraordinary our generation might be, we will never match our parents' heroism or their suffering. Our legacy is their extraordinary passion for life. Their fervor is our duty.

To be living anything short of moment-to-moment exultation while achieving momentous material success is considered blasphemy.

Passion vivre is our paradigm! I feel their unremitting judgment thrashing me.

Letter to Lizzie

Jerusalem
May 10, 1973

Dearest Lizzie,

I'm delighted to hear that you are so loved at your hotel! Even if Mom and Dad have not found the time to visit you, I am sure you have enough to occupy yourself. The new Ode to Rothko series you are working on sounds wonderful and ingenious, and needing the red of the paintings to be precisely the color of blood is so metaphysically metaphorical.

I've been giving your question regarding what I remember about our childhood some thought. And I will do whatever I can to jog my memory so that I can help you to regain yours. You've always accused me of being way too serious, so please bear that in mind as you read my recollections. I hope this story sheds some light on our world.

I remember the row you mentioned in your letter. That summer I went to Europe with Mom. Dad obviously could not join us because he had to stay behind and work, and someone needed to keep an eye on you. Being the bubblehead that you were, you had to attend summer school. I really would have preferred to go to camp, but over Dad's and my objections, Mom insisted that I accompany her.

Our first stop was two weeks in Paris with her cousin Ella; at that time, she lived in a townhouse on the Bois de Boulogne. Mom and I were given our own rooms. My cousin Andre's room was empty because he was off summer skiing in South America with his father: I slept there. Andre was a jazz freak who had put photographs of jazz musicians all over the walls. Each night for two weeks, I'd fall asleep looking at sweating black men blowing into horns.

The next place we went was Geneva. When we arrived, Mom announced that she had hired a guide to show me the city. The Swiss nerd wore thick glasses, a frumpy brown tweed suit, and brown orthopedic shoes that squeaked when she walked. She had bad breath, dandruff, and bored me to tears. In short, I couldn't wait to get back to the hotel.

When I returned, Mom was sitting at the mirror applying her makeup. Her hazel eyes and wavy, light brown hair were the kind of 1940s glamour that made her look like a movie star. Looking up at my reflection, she said, "I ran into a friend from work in the lobby this afternoon, isn't that a coincidence?"

"Who?" I asked.

"Oh, Dr. Schwarzkopf," she said.

I may have been twelve, but I knew this guy wasn't a friend; this coincidence was her boss.

"Oh, Mom," I chirped, "I've been meaning to ask

you, do people have to fuck to have children?"

Coolly, without looking up, she dabbed perfume behind each ear and said, "Yes, dear, why do you ask?"

"'Cause I think sex is really gross," I said. And turned around and walked into the bathroom.

The man from work was the head of pathology at Mount Sinai Hospital. He spoke barely above a whisper in a heavy German accent and always wore black. Black jeans, black polo shirt, black espadrilles, black Ray-Bans, black slicked-back hair. From Geneva on, we traveled together in his little black European rental car.

Mom and I always shared a hotel room. When we arrived in Lausanne, since we'd been driving all day and I was tired, I went to bed early. While I climbed into my pajamas, she dressed carefully in the new silk clothes she had purchased in Paris, and then went to dinner with the man who wore black. When she left, she locked the door behind her and took the key. I wondered what would happen if there were a fire. I went out on the terrace and checked to see whether I'd be able to climb over the rail to the room next door. It would be easy. And I could always yell. I was sure someone would come. Feeling reassured, I went to sleep.

When I awoke, the luminescent travel clock in the red leather case said three thirty. I was alone. I decided to wait up for her. I turned on the lights when I got tired of waiting in the dark, and there were black bugs all over the white walls. That totally freaked me out. So I turned the lights off and reluctantly went back to waiting in the dark.

By six that morning, the sun was up and the room was filled with light. I closed my eyes and pretended to be asleep while she tiptoed into the room. I watched her quietly undress and climb into bed.

We three traveled together for four weeks—two weeks in Switzerland and then on to Italy for another two weeks. We navigated the towns of Milano, Genoa, Nervi, and Santa Margherita, where when I walked down the street to the post office to mail my letters to Dad, the boys walking behind me would call me bella and whistle.

Finally there was Portofino. I loved Portofino, not only because it was our last stop, but because it was a picturesque port town filled with elegant little shops, cafés, and restaurants where I learned to eat spaghetti con pomodoro.

When the tide rises in Portofino, the streets flood with seawater and the women wear sandals with tall cork soles to prevent their feet from getting wet. Mom would rarely buy me clothes since I was growing, but in Portofino she bought me a pair of those sandals with cork soles that made me two inches taller. I loved wearing them; they made me feel pretty and grown-up.

I despised the doctor and mentioned Dad to him as often as possible. Mom tried to make me apologize, but I wouldn't. He wasn't my father, and he didn't belong with us. I felt as if our trip would never end.

Meal after meal, the whispering man in black really started getting on my nerves. I fantasized about killing them both with a big knife.

Finally, the day arrived. We were flying home on Lufthansa, alone.

But there had been some kind of outbreak and two planes had been quarantined, so Mom and I flew back to New York on Alitalia. Thank God, he had made his own travel arrangements. The ride home was very bumpy; the turbulence made me sick and I threw up in a paper bag. I couldn't understand anything anyone said to me because everyone on the flight spoke Italian. When we arrived at JFK Airport, no one was there to greet us.

Dad waited for us in the living room. When we entered, I ran to him and he hugged and kissed me hello. He smelled like aftershave and pipe tobacco. I told him how much I had missed him. He said he was happy that I was home, safe and sound. Mom was standing beside me, arms crossed, tapping her foot.

"Why weren't you at the airport to greet us?"

"Did you have to do it in front of the child?" he said.

"I don't know what you're talking about."

"You miserable whore!"

"Shut up!"

"Just like in the camps! Did you have to fuck another Nazi?"

I watched Mom remove her high-heeled shoe and run at Dad's face with the edge of the heel. I got out of the way. He caught her by her wrists and threw her down on the floor. She got up and ran for the telephone and asked the operator for the police. I started screaming, then I hid under the table. Dad ran over and ripped the phone out of her hand, hitting her in the head with the receiver. Mom fell backward, and for a moment she didn't move. I watched as Dad stood over her with the telephone receiver in his hand.

Then she moved.

"You don't know what the hell you're talking about!" she screamed.

"Your boss, you miserable cunt!"

"I swear I didn't sleep with him!"

She was up on her feet and came at Dad again, clawing at his face. He slapped her and threw her down on the floor, and then ran out of the house, slamming the door behind him.

Then it was very quiet, and neither I nor Mom moved for quite some time. I was under the dining room table with my arms wrapped around my knees, shaking. The only way to control the trembling was to quietly rock back and forth, muffling the tears running down my cheeks.

Mom picked herself up, straightened her clothes,

and put on her shoes. Then she lit a cigarette, poured herself a cognac, neat, and knocked it back in one shot. She brushed her hair, checked her makeup in the mirror, reapplied her lipstick, and said, "Come on out. Why are you hiding? Don't you want to go out for dinner? I want to eat a steak at Howard Johnson's. How about you?"

"Is Daddy coming back?" I asked.

"Maybe," she said. "Now is not the time to talk about that. Now is the time to eat. I'm ravenous."

"I'm not hungry," I said, "and I want to see Grandma."

"You'll see her tomorrow. Come," she said, as she held out her hand, "we're going."

I wanted to grasp it. But I was afraid of what she would do to me when she realized that I had been the one to send Dad the letter telling him about the creepy German doctor who only wore black.

Hope that helps.
Love, Ta Bête
XOXOXOXOXO   Bette

Chapter 7

A Dream

Jerusalem
May 15, 1973

I am lying in bed where I am being smothered by a weight I cannot see; the weight of a million tons is bearing down upon me like a giant press, as if I were a grape being squeezed for my juice. I moan loudly in my sleep, and the cry wakes me.

As my eyes adjust to the darkness, I realize that I am lying in bed drenched in sweat, that I have been dreaming, again. The cat lies motionless beside me. My moaning does not appear to have startled him.

My eyelids are so heavy, I can barely keep my eyes open. Lashes flutter briefly and close like a metal safe. I fall asleep and the pressing begins again.

I awake this time with a start. Now I am afraid to fall asleep, afraid that I will be crushed. The desire for sleep continues, alongside the fear that I will die if I fall asleep. Intuitively, I understand that there is a spirit in the house that can find no peace, a spirit who has died so horribly that he cannot let go of this place. Having had the insight, I address the spirit out loud. I can feel his presence. He is angry. I explain I am only passing through, that I will remain in the house just a short time, that I am moving on and my living in this house is for only a little while longer. I say that I am sorry for his pain, sorry for whatever life did to him, and ask that he tolerate my presence; I mean him no harm and I will not interfere with him. The cat does not move while I deliver this monologue, but rather is strangely subdued.

Spiritualists believe that a soul's presence in a room feels icy, but this presence produces heat. The temperature in the room goes up twenty-five degrees. I kick off the covers. I cover myself with a sheet and a cotton coverlet. I am afraid. I cradle myself in my own arms, rocking back and forth, and hide in a place deep within myself.

Diary Entry

Jerusalem
May 25, 1973

The cocktail party took place at my high school classmate Jane's family's apartment on Park Avenue. Many of the guests were also graduates of Columbia Grammar. Ginny Gordon was there wearing the uniform: Gucci loafers, Hermes scarf, and Louis Vuitton handbag. We were all standing around drinking champagne while the young men discussed the weight of being the third generation to attend Yale. I stood next to Chip, a gorgeous, tall, blond surfer type. Lizzie's former beau and younger man, Andreas, was there, the German with the intense eyes and matching personality, the fellow she should have married instead of Peter.

Unlike my sister's romantic relationship, my friendship with Andreas consisted of my cheering him on at soccer games while he allowed me to cheat in biology class.

As they spoke, Chip nursed a Bloody Mary that he held in his left hand while with his right, he continually tapped the crest on his blazer pocket, as if he feared it might fall off. As he lifted the glass to his lips, I watched carefully to see whether the celery stalk would go up his nose, since his nostrils flared to twice their normal size when he sipped.

We acknowledged the massive yet tasteful flower arrangements, applauded our attractive hostess's impeccable taste in all things. We secretly admitted that we envied her friends and the places they summered. We agreed that being an icon of respectability had its responsibilities. As future world leaders, we further agreed that generation upon generation of Bonesmen had a duty to go to the best schools. Suddenly, Andreas turned to me and said, "I know you've told me, but where did your grandparents go to college?"

At that moment, I could have lied, I could have been charming and feminine, I could have pretended to be dumb or drunk or utterly stupid, I could have needed to powder my nose and freshen my lipstick, but instead, I said, "My grandparents were 'exterminated' at Treblinka."

Andreas smiled, as if he'd known all along that I would fall into the trap. Chip remembered something he just had to do on the other side of the room. In his haste, he ran smack into the most boring woman at the party (served him right), who at that moment was hugging the punch bowl a bit too tightly. Yet he knew that even in her inebriated state, she would know better than to be so gauche as to mention something as deeply offensive as the Holocaust at a cocktail party.

On the other hand, I could not understand why the subject had so offended him, when, after all, they were my grandparents who were murdered and most definitely not his. I turned to ask him, and to my surprise Andreas had disappeared into the crowd.

I stood alone pretending to ignore my desertion, high heels rooted in the expensive oriental rug, slowly sipping the champagne growing warm in Jane's magnificent crystal glasses while feigning contemplation of the Renoir trapped in a massive gilt frame hanging over the piano that no one in the house knew how to play. Original Renoirs don't come cheap, you know. It was then that I began pondering whether the money Jane's grandfather had made was earned on the board of *IG Farben, Standard Oil, ITT,* or *IBM*. Or had the Renoir been a gift, perhaps, for a job well done? The irony that I, a direct descendant of the very slave labor force that might very well have facilitated my hosts' ability to afford the unaffordable, was sipping champagne with the offspring of my grandparents' killers struck me as hilarious. And I started to laugh uncontrollably all by myself, and I laughed and laughed as if I were all alone in the room. No one noticed.

Jane's family photos were prominently displayed on the shiny lid of the closed piano, sheathed in identical silver frames purchased in bulk from Tiffany's. Her sister had recently been married and the wedding party shot stood at the center. Since the bride was in the grade above mine, and just below Lizzie's, we had not expected to be among the included. I leaned over to get a better look at the details of her wedding gown, and noticed that, lo and behold, Jenny looked a little thick through the middle. It was then that it occurred to me that the impromptu yet spectacular wedding at the Pierre had occurred so magically because Jenny was pregnant! I looked around the room. She wasn't there. What about all the smiling, happy photos in the New York Times? Maybe they were smiling because the groom had agreed to marry her!

At that moment, Jane walked over to say that she did not believe in either love or divorce; she felt that both were unreliable. She insisted she was a bottom-line kind of gal, and good-naturedly accused me of daydreaming about the perfect romantic soul mate, when what she felt I should be seeking out was a strong financial match.

She'd just gotten engaged to a Wall Streeter, and the light reflecting off the diamond of her engagement ring was blinding everyone in the room. When I gawked at the size of the stone, shielding my eyes, she leaned over and whispered in my ear that if her marriage did not work out, she would simply drink herself into oblivion on the best champagne and snort the occasional line and just get on with it. What did it all matter, anyway?

She was just doing what was expected.

As she spoke, I could not determine whether I was experiencing a rush of envy, or had just had too much to drink. I asked her, why had she been born into her life and not mine? She replied, the fact that I spent my days questioning the very foundations she took so completely for granted would have made her life for me quite difficult, didn't I think? I had to agree.

I didn't know exactly what I wanted, but I knew without a doubt that I didn't want her life. Which was a good thing, seeing that God, for lack of a better word, had seen to it that that would never be an issue. I don't remember much else about that evening, it became lost in a blur of powdered white lines and champagne.

I do recall, however, sometime later, standing in our parents' living room, a mere three blocks away. There was my mother's Chickering piano, surrounded by bookcases filled with hardcover art books, which leaned against those of Elie Wiesel and Primo Levi. Treblinka, The Rise and Fall of the Third Reich, Mila 18, The Young Lions, and Exodus. Conspicuously absent were leather-bound Harvard Classics and family photos in silver Tiffany frames.

I again became a small child in that room. Mom was playing the piano, beneath which I sat on the bare parquet floor listening and watching her feet press the pedals, as I drew pictures of trees and flowers on large pieces of newsprint, an open coffee tin at my knee overflowing with pastels.

Mom was playing Chopin, as she often did. I was humming along with a particularly sad etude when I started to cry. Suddenly, Mom stopped playing and started to scream. I mean, scream as if someone had just ripped her heart out. I ran out of the house holding my ears.

Chapter 8

Letter to Lizzie

Jerusalem
May 26, 1973

Dearest Lizzie,

I haven't heard back from you, and I hope that is a
good sign. I do worry, so please respond when you get
a minute. The memories are starting to come quickly,
so I am writing them down and sending them off to
you as they pour out of me.

All day I've been thinking about the Eichmann
trial. It's 1961 and we're sitting in the living room hud-
dled in front of the black-and-white television set. Eichmann is being questioned. Then the other Nazis who
worked with him are questioned as well.

"Do you remember a conversation you had with
the defendant regarding a Jewish child in his employ?
A young man who was beaten to death? Do you remember the circumstances surrounding that situation?
How did it come to pass?"*

And Eichmann sitting in his glass box looking
bored, his hands fidgeting while his stone face re-

* Taken from actual testimony of the Eichmann trial.

mained impassive behind those glasses.

After a while, I stopped keeping track of the testimony. I always assumed that because you were older, you understood what was happening. I hated being forced to watch the trial. And the evidence, the black-and-white photographs of bodies piled high, knowing that Mom and Grandma and Sylvia were imagining everyone they knew among the bodies. I was frightened by Grandma's weeping and moaning as she rocked back and forth.

And then, as if nothing remarkable had happened, the television would be turned off, and I'd be sent to bed where I'd lie for hours, imagining holiday dinners with twenty or thirty or even forty family members sitting around a beautifully appointed table, covered in starched linens, polished silver, and sparkling crystal. Relatives chatting warmly and happily, relatives I had never known who resembled one another and looked a lot like Mom and Dad.

In my reveries, there was never food on the plates or wine in the glasses, as if Sholem Aleichem's character Bonscha Schweig had been the caterer; penniless and utterly silent, the beauty of Bonscha was his infinite humility, his immeasurable poverty, his ineffable sensitivity and sense of utter worthlessness. He was a man whose spirit was so unreservedly broken that in the course of an entire lifetime he was incapable of articulating a single sound.

When he died, he went to heaven, where he was welcomed by God and offered a reward for his suffering. God was willing to realize his greatest desires. So, for what does poor Bonscha ask? Through tears of gratitude streaming down his face, he speaks for the first time, and requests a warm buttered roll each morning for breakfast. The story of Bonscha Schweig has always made me want to kill myself.

There is a museum here called Yad Vashem. I went there with a group of American volunteers from the kibbutz. I had never been to a "Holocaust" museum before.

When you walk in, there are floor-to-ceiling, life-sized black-and-white photographs, like the ones Margaret Bourke-White took at the liberation of the camps. Larger-than-life-sized photographs of skeletal Jews with hollow eyes, wearing striped prison uniforms, caps, and wooden shoes, looking through the barbed wire like animals in a zoo.

Their eyes look directly into yours. The effect is unnerving.

The photos were taken by the Nazis; yet one more testament to their obsessive/compulsive need to document each and every detail of their self-aggrandizement. The temperature outside may have been a hundred degrees, but I stood still, immobilized by the room's tomb-ness; I was surrounded by the dead. I could do nothing but gaze into the desperation in each pair of eyes. It was as if I'd been plunged into a bathtub filled with ice water and Dr. Mengele stood beside me with a stopwatch, timing me, to see how long I would take to freeze. I stood that way seemingly for hours, my heart shattered.

This *could have been* me. This is me. This is what I *come* from. *How can a human being come from this?*

When my classmates in America talked about growing up in the same house as their great-great-grandparents; when they bragged about their hearty Puritan stock and nonchalantly mentioned in a tone mimicking humility that they would never really have to work, so their lives could be devoted to helping others, or driving race cars, or attending parties, I was rendered speechless.

How was it that I did not comprehend, until this moment, how utterly bereft I have felt? My parents spared me the knowledge of how significantly their world had been destroyed; a world in which I too would have been born in my great-great- grandfather's house, and would have lived the life of a great-grand-child of philanthropists, with all the respect that a descendant of a pillar of the community commands.

That night, I slept at the kibbutz. In the early morning, I dreamt that the socialist farm community had been turned into a concentration camp and we were being rounded up for extermination. I heard women and children screaming and crying, and I awoke in terror. Only when I got my bearings did I realize that the screaming I had heard in my dream had actually been the roosters crowing.

Later that day, on the way home to Jerusalem, I decided to take a sherut from the central bus station in Tel Aviv. A sherut is a shared taxi, usually an enormous Mercedes, which costs little more than a bus, but is much faster and far more comfortable. People stagger in and sit down, then they ask the driver the price of the trip. There is much whimsy involved in determining the price; it is not necessarily the same for everyone, and everything is negotiable. For example, I speak Hebrew, and most Israelis tell me that my accent sounds Swedish. The driver usually asks whether I am a student. When I explain that I study art at Bezalel, most drivers are pleased that I am studying in their country and not America, so they offer a half-price student discount. On this trip, however, I was asked to pay the full price.

After ten minutes, there was still one seat left. So we waited, and it seemed that everyone's patience was growing thin. Finally, a young German tourist carrying a backpack got in, and in English he asked, "How much?" The driver immediately charged him double. And without question, the young man paid it.

At first, everyone in the taxi stole sidelong glances at one another, but said nothing. Then, a robust woman in the front seat next to the driver spoke up and accused him of overcharging the young man. It did not take long for there to be a complete uproar in which every passenger had an opinion he made known. One man said that after what the Germans did to us, the kid should pay triple; that he had gotten off easy. Another said that the child was not responsible for what his parents or grandparents had done; that one should give him credit for being here, a visitor in Israel; that we had to see that he was different. The accusations and recriminations went on for forty minutes, all in Hebrew, while the nineteen-year-old sat looking out the window.

The trip to Jerusalem usually takes an hour. We were nearing the outskirts of the city, and finally the driver conceded, deciding to reimburse the student half of what he had charged him. I was the one elected to explain the misunderstanding.

I decided to speak to him in English; I could not bring myself to explain what had happened in German. Confused, my sentiments were caught somewhere in between. It was true that he was not responsible for what had happened, but we had to bear the brunt of the war by being homeless and family-less. It seemed only fair that he should have to pay as well.

I'll admit, I didn't say that. I just told him that the driver had tried to overcharge him and the rest of the passengers were outraged, and left it at that. He thanked me, and when we arrived in Jerusalem, I couldn't wait to get away.

I walked home rather than take a crowded bus. Besides, the sun was setting, and the city was caught in the magical instant between day and night; streetlamps were twinkling noisily, radios were blaring Arabic music and Israeli newscasts, the hadashim of the day were pouring out of the open windows like hot lava dripping off the balconies and into the street.

I couldn't get the images of Yad Vashem out of my head. As I reached the turquoise gate, I started to shake uncontrollably. I managed to drag myself to the garden outside my studio, where I fell to my knees.

Many hours later I had not moved from that spot and was beginning to feel numb. Gazing up at the night sky, I searched for a bright Venus to lift my spirit, but a mist had settled on the hillside. The stars sparkled somewhere beyond, and I was transported into another mist, one that enveloped the train upon which Mom and I had traveled from Paris to Munich during the summer of 1963.

Our mother's cousin, Ella, had taken us to the train station in Paris.

We had spent two weeks living with her, seeing the sights while living in her rambling beaux arts townhouse where she seemed to spend entirely too much time alone. Waving on the foggy platform as the train pulled out, she looked just like a character out of a Hitchcock movie. Ella had golden blonde hair that was always perfectly coiffed. Always terribly chic, she wore a pink Chanel suit with black piping and carried a Hermes bag. She looked like a cross between the French film star, Simone Signoret, and Grace Kelly, which she used entirely to her advantage by enticing younger men and gigolos to the house when her husband and son were out of town.

Mom wore a suit just like hers in black and white, and I had been told in no uncertain terms that on this trip I was to wear a skirt.

We had a private compartment with red velvet seats and wood paneling. We were traveling to Munich to visit Mom's friend from before the war, Berta Honig. We spent the afternoon eating lunch in a very elegant dining car, and afterward went back to our couchette for a nap.

When we crossed the border into Germany, you could tell that you weren't in France anymore. There was shouting. Mom and I looked out the window. The German border police were all wearing black leather trench coats, black breeches, shiny black leather boots that reached their knees, black jackets beneath the trench coats, and black leather caps. Some of them had German shepherd dogs on leashes. Mom turned to me, her face pale, and said, "Bettylein, don't be afraid."

Within moments, the door to our compartment flew open and a tall, good-looking officer walked through. He clicked his heels, saluted, and in German asked for our passports. Mom opened her bag, took out our passports and handed them to the officer, while I sat on the red velvet seat watching him. He looked at our passport photos, then up at us. Slamming closed the passports, he returned them with what seemed a bit too much fanfare.

"*Cigaretten?*" he barked. (Cigarettes?)

Mom explained in German that she had purchased the amount allowed in the duty-free shop, and showed him the boxes of Marlboros sitting in a plastic duty-free bag next to our luggage on the overhead rack.

He stared at her. Then he grabbed the pocketbook out of her hands and started rifling through it. She responded like lightning, slapping him twice across the face, making sure the ring on her right hand scraped his cheek. Then she started screaming at the top of her lungs, "*Verdamter Nazi! Hast mich nicht im krieg umgebracht, und wierst mich jesz nicht humilieren!*" (You damned Nazi, you didn't kill me during the war, and you won't humiliate me now!)

He touched his cheek with his index finger to see whether or not he was bleeding. He looked as if he was debating whether or not to slap her back. Luckily, within seconds the car was filled with people.

They all looked alike. Most had removed their hats, which were now tucked under their arms. There was an overwhelming amount of black leather jammed together. I sat eye-level with numerous black crotches and suede knee pads. There was very little air. The sound of barking dogs straining at their leashes played as background music to the more palpable hum of whispered apologies; men's voices assuming a special tone of calm. They spoke to her as if she were a mad-woman. They were explaining, in the nicest way of course, that she would have to calm down.

At any moment, I expected them to tackle her to the floor and administer an injection just to shut her up.

"Sons of bitches," she said out loud. "If anyone ever calls you a kike, you have my permission to beat the shit out of them, do you understand?"

"Yes, Mom."

"I didn't survive the war to have these sons of bitches start the same bullshit again. Not as long as I live. Don't ever let them make you feel afraid to be a Jew. And if they try, you teach them that they can't. Okay?"

"Okay."

My heart thundered in my ears.

The black swarm slowly evacuated the cave like a team of Draculas; they folded themselves up and dis-persed. We were not disturbed again. When we reached sunny Munich, the officers who had ridden with us were careful to remove their hats when they saw us.

That fall, when we returned to school, the new

one where we had to wear those scratchy gray wool skirts and navy blue blazers, during a break one morning Becky Sands, a classmate, called me a "disgusting kike." Without thinking, I socked her in the nose and threw her against the blackboard. I wanted to kill her. Her nose started spraying blood. She ran out of the room crying and threatened to get me expelled from school.

Of course, I was hauled into the principal's office and had to wait until Mom came to get me. When she arrived, she was wearing the same suit she had worn on the trip to Munich, her hair was done, and her nails had been freshly polished a dark red.

She walked into the office where I sat across from the principal. Beside me, there was an empty chair prepared for her. She looked at me, patted my head, smoothed my hair, and sat down.

"What seems to be the problem?" she asked.

"It seems your daughter got into a fight."

She shot a glance at me, then quietly looked down at the purse on her lap. Slowly, she opened it and took out a cigarette. Then she held it in her hand and leaned forward as if asking the principal to light it.

Without saying a word, he reached into his pocket and produced an expensive gold lighter. Then, extending his arm across the desk, he lit her cigarette. She inhaled and looked away, settling into her chair. She did not thank him.

He seemed to be waiting for some sort of acknowledgment, and when none seemed forthcoming, he pushed a cut crystal ashtray across the desk toward her, leaving a trail on the leather top.

"What was the fight about?" she finally asked.

"Her classmate called her a kike and she responded by giving her a bloody nose."

Mom threw her head back and laughed. She looked beautiful.

"That's all right," she said, flicking her ash into the ashtray, "she has my permission to do that. I didn't survive the Holocaust so that some ignorant little anti-Semite could degrade my child. I told her she has my permission to beat the shit out of anyone who dares to call her a kike. We fought back too late. That will never happen to her."

"I see."

"Do you?"

"Yes."

"Good."

The room became very quiet. No one spoke for several moments. I looked from one to the other. The principal finally broke the silence.

"She's had quite a day. Perhaps she'd like to go home with you now?"

We got up together and the principal held the door to his office open for us. We walked out into the sunlight on Lexington Avenue and 70th Street.

"So, is the little brat afraid of you now?" she asked.

"Terrified."

"Good. I'm proud of you. Why don't we go to Rumplemeyer's for some hot chocolate?"

Mom was so happy. We walked down Fifth Avenue along the park, and then up 57th Street to Rumplemeyer's. On a weekday afternoon in the sunshine.

I'm so very tired, and going to sleep. I have a slew of new rolls of film I need to develop tomorrow. Perhaps in my next letter, I'll send a contact sheet so you can see what I'm working on.

Keep enjoying those designer drugs.

Love, XOXOXOXOXOXOXO Ta Bête, La Bette

Illusion of Memory

Chapter 9

Letter to La Bette

The Grand Hotel du Mal
Californ-I-Ay
June 1, 1973

My dearest Monkey-Head,

I have seen another world. I don't mean I got on a plane and went to Outer Mongolia, either. I saw another world without leaving this house. It happened three days ago, when we were sipping cocktails as per usual. I was enjoying our conversation when I heard voices. The voices of children playing, but I knew there weren't any children residing in the hotel. So I followed the voices and was led to the kitchen. I walked around the kitchen trying to locate the source of the voices. I noticed that when I passed the refrigerator where the milk, butter, and eggs were kept, the voices became stronger.

I sat nearby and closed my eyes and listened. I realized that sounds were traveling along the cord that went from the refrigerator to the wall socket. I heard two men: a father and a grandfather. And band music, the kind you hear at parades. I was so excited!

I wanted to know who these people were, so I just asked them. You can't imagine what happened next.

The father did most of the talking. He said they had lived in the house prior to the present tenants, before it was a hotel. He came from a huge family and had grown up in the house with five brothers and a sister, who were all grown and married with children of their own. When I asked him where they were living, he said they were dead and buried in the woods behind the house in a small family cemetery. Dead? I said. That can't be. You must be mistaken. You must be alive somewhere in this house, I said. Well, yes, he answered. We are alive, but not in the way that you are accustomed to thinking about life. Well, I asked, where are you? To which he said, we are here in the fourth dimension. There is a thin veil between worlds. I asked, how do I get into the fourth dimension? I mean, I could hear them! Why couldn't I see them?

So he walked me through it. He told me to sit down in the lotus position, close my eyes, and get centered. He said to breathe deeply and invite the spirit world to open my eyes. He said that when I opened my eyes I would meet the entire family.

I did this, concentrating very hard, for about ten minutes. When I opened my eyes, there standing before me was the man I had just heard on the electrical wire, and he was so handsome! He was about six foot three, with blond hair and blue eyes, and by his side were his three beautiful blond-haired sons, and the grandfather, a very dignified country gentleman with a full head of silver hair, wearing tweeds and smoking a pipe of cherry tobacco.

I asked about the mother, and they said that she refused to return to the house; that she believed the house was cursed and she'd never return. But they just laughed and said she was superstitious, and it was her loss; that they preferred to remain in the house because they had built it and so many things had happened in that house which they didn't want to let go of marriages and births and parties and holidays.

They gave me the grand tour of the house and even showed me what it used to look like prior to its being converted into a hotel! Oh my. They must have been so rich, Monkey-Head. The house was sumptuous; the rooms all had exquisite velvet drapes and sheer silk curtains, and were piled high with furniture from all over the world—pieces they had brought back from their travels to the most exotic places. Venetian glass mirrors and chandeliers and deep red and green Venetian silks lining the walls.

Then they invited me to dine with them. A nanny appeared and the boys went to bed, leaving the father and grandfather as my dinner companions. There was a cook, of course, who was from India, and oh the curries that followed one after the other, accompanied by saffron rice and chutneys made of exotic fruits, and chilled champagne, and more champagne, until we thought we would burst from pleasure.

We retired to the card room and played hearts until the sun rose, and I'm afraid I played miserably and lost by a landslide, but the two men were so utterly entertaining and gentlemanly that I didn't mind. We parted company at six thirty.

I tiptoed back to my room and fell into a deep and satisfying sleep. When I awoke, I knew that we would never die. I knew it in my bones. I have discovered a whole other level of existence right here, now.

You must come and visit so that I can show you what I've seen.

Yours forever,
Lizzie the Lover

Chapter 10

Diary Entry

Jerusalem
King David Hotel
June 3, 1973

Yesterday, while sunbathing at the King David Hotel, I saw the guy from the Mossad, the one who likes to pick up American girls. He's adorable, in a Kirk Douglas sort of way, and a total gossip monger. He was busy spreading rumors that President Nixon had been recruiting Nazis, not only into the CIA, but into the Republican Party, all in the hope of getting lucky with this right-wing American girl. He's the kind of guy who would marry an American for a green card without telling her. Now he's just scoping out the territory to see who will go for the bait.

I happen to know he deals in arms.

"Who do you deal arms to?" I asked.

"I sell to whoever will buy."

"Why?"

"Because if I don't, someone else will."

Hmmm. That was obvious. He had so much negative energy. I decided I needed to get away from him. So I walked to the newspaper stand and started flipping through American magazines. The local ex-pat paper is the Jerusalem Post. Their style gets pretty old, so each week I like to pick up copies of Time and Newsweek and read them while sitting poolside. Time magazine had a painting of Sadat on the cover, painted by my former anatomy teacher, Audrey Flack.

This week there were more bodyguards than usual. Then I read that Nancy Kissinger and her enormous feet were supposed to arrive for peace talks. Then I looked up and saw those very feet five inches away from where I was sitting, resplendent in the grass, and suddenly I understood the reason for the additional goons.

It's always hot, but today it's particularly hot, so I get up again to get a cold Orangina, placing my towel in a strategic spot, and when I return, I cross my legs and wait to see what will happen. I light a cigarette and peer out from beneath my aviator shades. Occasionally I look down at the magazine on my lap and examine the photographs of civil rights workers in Alabama or read a story about Henry Kissinger's upcoming visit to Jerusalem.

Then I look around. The Watergate scandal makes for great entertainment fodder here. All the internationals sit around the pool swapping info and laughing each time there is a new development. I don't find it quite so amusing. And I wonder, was there ever a time the world was not on fire?

I knew after seeing the female soldier's smile on the cover of *LIFE Magazine*, that I was destined to be here in this mysterious place, the place our only living grandmother referred to as Palestina and Dad considered a glorified ghetto.

When I contacted the Jewish Agency on Park Avenue, I was assigned to a kibbutz in the Negev desert, and told that I'd be weeding green peppers, picking grapefruits, and packing peaches in 120 degrees Fahrenheit. My heart was filled with joy.

The world might be on fire, but I felt safe. I was surrounded by so many gorgeous Israeli soldiers and Mossad operatives, all lined up to protect us.

Illusion of Memory

Letter to Bette

The Grand Hotel du Mal
Rural California
June 5, 1973

Dearest Itsy Bitsy Betsy,

Darling, you really are having the most enlighten-
ing life experiences! Witnessing Mossad operatives is
about as dramatic as life gets. I still have copies of the
article you sent about the Lod Airport shoot-out where
twenty-six innocent people were slaughtered in an act
of revenge by those three Japanese terrorists carrying
violin cases with submachine guns inside. The scene
was like something out of a Scorsese movie, I mean g-r-
i-t-t-y! You must run over there and photograph the
scene the way it is today and immediately send me the
photos of the bullet holes left in the walls. I'll use the
image in my next painting. Perhaps, if you don't mind
of course, I'd create a Pollock-like experiential piece of
blood-splattered walls. People will stand before it, a totally abstract image in the exact shade of blood of the
deceased and those bullet holes, and they will be reduced to tears. Can you imagine that? Only art can do
that. And by the way, all that stuff about the camps, I
find it so depressing. Except for the black leather, of
course. Don't go on about that if you don't mind, it up-

sets me.

We had the most divine party last weekend. It began with cocktails on the veranda, champagne laced with LSD, and really, in about an hour we were all in outer space. I found myself looking at the night sky, gawking at the millions of stars, awestruck, speechless. How mysterious is this world, and how small and insignificant we are. And the things we do? Utterly meaningless. Laughable. Oh, the way we blow ourselves up and strut around! Just thinking about my own posturing reduced me to tears. I've never laughed so hard.

About halfway through the evening, an orgy began. I don't remember how it started, or who initiated it, but I found myself quite engaged! We became an amorphous organism, grinding and howling and laughing and screaming, a symphony of sucking and licking noises, with the occasional slap as percussion keeping time while the screamers played their leading roles, and the secondary players groaned theirs. The event had a real theatricality to it, a lightness that reminded me of the opera Der Rosenkavalier by Strauss: doors slamming, women falling in love with women pretending to be men, then realizing their error, and falling in love with them anyway, and men pretending to be men, when really they were women. In the end, after everyone had tried everyone and everything, we simply lay on the floor in a heap, waiting for the sun to rise.

It did, of course, the weather being so damn predictable on the West Coast. Then we went through all the clothes lying on the floor, sorted through the lot, choosing whatever we pleased, reinventing ourselves on the spot. I mean, who cares whose clothes they were? And the operative word is *were*.

Afterward we went for a walk on the grounds, naming the birds with completely new names that we made up, while watching the sky change, still holding hands, arms draped around one another.

I am in love with life, in love with the feel of my own body, in love with skin and bone, muscle and hair. The others, whom I barely tolerate on a daily basis, become the containers that fill me. By their touch, I am transformed into starlight, rolling my naked body in the damp earth, swimming on the surface of the moon. All the next day I saw flashes of things.

Fingers. A tongue.

Memory is the pit into which you want me to fall.

I won't. Go to what you fear, you will say, I know you. I fear that when I fall, that I will sink into the abyss forever. Because once I know a truth, I must embrace it, the wound from which all creativity springs, the wound into which I crawl, belly first, hurling the covers over my head. Don't tell me!

Remember for me? Ach, such silliness.

Did I mention there is a most interesting, life-sized

cat here from a very prominent White Russian family, who visits me nightly? His name is Prince Stephanovich, and because he was born here, as opposed to his native Russia, his papers say he is a Maine Coon Cat. He has enormous...um...fur, huge green eyes, and a soft beige belly the color of sand. We make mad love, he caresses me with his rough tongue, and afterward we lie together in the firelight while I read to him from Proust's *Remembrance of Things Past*.

He speaks fluent Russian and French of course, and we often discuss Dostoyevsky and Gogol late into the night. He has that impassioned, brooding, romantic nature the Russians are so famous for. I tell him that he may refer to himself as a Maine Coon, but I know his soul is that of a Wild Russian Forest Cat! What style, what flair! What brilliance! What fur!

> Your most loving,
> Lizalyonevskaya

Chapter 11

Letter to Bette

New York City
June 12, 1973

My dearest Bettylein,

Thank you for all your letters. As you know, Mom
has been ill.

It seems to all have come at once, and your aunt
Sylvia has been helping out around the house. Since
she is a dental hygienist, I thought it best that she take
care of Mom.

They had to remove Mom's right breast. The operation has made her very tired and very depressed. The
sooner you return home, the better.

There is only you now. Grandma is too old, Sylvia
has to go back to work, and I can't take any more time
away from my job.

Please let me know how soon you can plan your
trip home. That way, I can pick you up from the airport. Mom has asked me to tell you that she'll get you
an apartment of your own if you come back sooner. I
know that you and your mother have had your difficulties, but sometimes in a family you have to let go of

those differences. She would do it for you, you can be certain.

I am eager to see your paintings and your photographs. Take them off the stretchers and mail them home, or ask your friend Ehud who works for El Al to carry them as his luggage the next time he flies to NYC.

I miss you and look forward to seeing you again after all this time.

Love,
Dad

Letter to Dad

Jerusalem
June 22, 1973

Dearest Dad,

Hi. Your daughter has almost finished her master's degree. I'm happy to say that I'm in the process of completing the last two paintings.

I'm so sorry to hear about all the difficulties at home. I tried to speak to Mom in the hospital, but Sylvia wouldn't let me talk to her for more than two minutes, and they both seemed so irritable.

As for me, I met a very nice guy, someone I like a lot. He took me to Beersheba to meet his father, who is a lovely, quiet, humble Polish man who made me feel totally at home. It's remarkable; he lives alone in a small stucco house in the middle of the desert surrounded by grass and fruit trees, and he has planted his own vegetable garden. He eats what he grows. He seems peaceful and happy.

Unfortunately, the relationship between Amos and me doesn't seem meant to be. I'm starting to believe that I'm not very good at relationships. This time, I am heartbroken.

But life goes on. I'll be home before you know it, and the two years that I've lived here will seem like a blur.

I had Shabbat dinner with your college friend, Mr. Laron, and his family this past weekend. His son is still stationed at Kibbutz Revivim, where I've been living on the weekends. He will remain there for the next year. They all send you their warmest regards and want to know when you plan to visit.

Love,
Your Bettylein

Diary Entry

Jerusalem
June 23, 1973

My garden is in bloom. The fragrance of pomegranates, oranges, and apricots wafts in through the bedroom window in the early morning, while farther down the road, the olive trees are starting to blush.

Yesterday, Carlos, the Peruvian painter, and I walked to the Old City for lunch. It's quite a hike from where I live, but we hardly felt the distance.

We talked all the while about Correlations, a design theory being taught at the art and design school in Jerusalem by an American, which is very popular at the moment. It's pretty heady stuff, mathematical, not my strong suit. Sort of the antithesis of what I do. But we chatted about it nevertheless. When we arrived at the gate to the Old City, the combination of heat, light, and the intense aroma of the spices from the market took over and we continued walking for a time in silence.

The colorful djellabas were hanging in the stalls; the glistening Arabic silver jewelry was displayed in the windows. Before you see them, the intense smell of recently skinned sheepskin jars the senses. Wildly colored skins, they look as if the Tartars flew across the plains on their Arabian horses to deliver them. Cafés overflow with men playing shesh besh (backgammon) while they drink thick, sweet mint tea from small, gilt-edged Moroccan glasses, or black coffee in miniature cups, a hashish-filled hookah smoldering, the nozzle never far from reach.

Carlos led me down a maze of small streets paved with prehistoric cobblestones, stone houses standing silent, except for the buzz of large green flies mating in the heat. From somewhere, the sound of Arabic music blared over a transistor radio, filling the motionless air. We followed the sound down two steep limestone steps into a small, impeccably clean room with a white tiled floor, whitewashed walls, a rotating ceiling fan, and four small tables with wooden chairs.

Behind the counter in what looked like a pit stood a man wearing a red fez and a white, high-necked dress, grinding chickpeas, oil, and garlic into a paste using a white marble pestle. Hummus. Behind him was an oven, not unlike a small pizza oven, that contained baking pita breads. We stood in the doorway, bathed in the aroma of freshly baked bread.

In one corner of the room, four Arab men sat eating hummus and fuul, a similar paste made from lima beans. As we entered, they were wiping their plates clean with the last of their bread. They looked up, then one of the four shouted to the cook.

Carlos speaks Arabic. He said they were asking for mint tea to be brought to the table. The fez wearer nodded, shooing away the occasional fly with his left hand, while continuing to mash the chickpeas in a bowl with his right.

For a foray into the Old City, a woman's body must be covered. We do it out of respect for the Muslim culture, and because we've been told that Middle Eastern men have poor impulse control. For example, if you were to walk through the Arab market wearing shorts and a T-shirt without a bra, you'd be signaling to all the men that you were available to be used.

They were taught from childhood that European women were worthless creatures. Traveling through the religious Jewish neighborhoods of Rehavia and Mea Sharim was somewhat similar, in that their women were covered at all times, and even shaved their heads and wore wigs. Women wearing long, exposed tresses, combed loose to the waist, accompanied by tanned bare arms and legs, would find their bottoms caressed by a single sensuous hand, while the Hasid responsible would be busily twirling his payes with the other.

On this bright one-hundred-degree day, I wore jeans and a long-sleeved Arabic shirt open at the neck. Carlos whispered in English that it would be best if he ordered for me. We agreed on hummus with sesame paste known as tahini, and harif, a spicy oil made out of chilies, placed in the center, like a bloody bull's-eye. The heat demanded an ice-cold beer as an accompaniment.

From our seats, we watched the man in the fez

prepare our meals. Then, he took several fresh pitas out of the oven, piled six of them on a clean plate, and using a can opener hanging on an old piece of string, he popped open the beers. The sound made me laugh. Heads turned in my direction. Carlos paid, then quickly brought the food and drinks to the table.

The hummus was smooth, the pita bread soft and warm, yet crisp, and when swirled onto the bread, the garlic and red chilies of the spicy harif burst on the tongue. The beer was remarkably icy. Drinking the beer straight out of the bottle, we ate slowly, savoring the flavors.

Tipping my head back for a sip of beer, I'd count the numerous flypapers covered with dead flies hanging from the ceiling. After a while, I started counting them. A recent captive was struggling desperately to break free, but the more he struggled, the more stuck he became.

Despite the heat of the oven, the room was cool. The stone walls gave off an earthy dampness. The fez-wearing cook turned up the music on the radio as if the tune was a favorite of his.

"I have a friend who is Palestinian," said Carlos, raising his voice. "He's a writer. I'd like you to meet him."

"I don't think I've ever met a Palestinian," I said, "not knowingly, anyway."

"He hangs out at a café around the corner. We'll go

there for dessert."

Then raising his voice to a shout, he said,

"They have the best baklava and Arabic coffee made with hell (cardamom seeds). The café attracts artists and people who like to talk politics. It's the kind of place where you can drink a single coffee all day, or sit with one Ouzo or a glass of water and engage in friendly and, at times, high-pitched banter with people from all over the world. Where else are you going to find a painter from Peru, an American collagist, and a Palestinian writer sitting together and speaking in a civilized manner?"

Chapter 12

Diary Entry

Jerusalem
June 30, 1973

A Dream

I am floating in warm fluid. From what seems like another room, I can hear the sound of muffled voices.

"I'm not ready!" she screams. "I will die if I have children."

"You're being dramatic," he says.

"If you make me have this child, I'll kill myself!"

"If you don't have this child, I'll divorce you and leave you in Germany."

I'm swaying to and fro, as if I were in a hammock. At moments I feel engulfed by something that makes me laugh and then hiccup. Sometimes, the berth in which I lie becomes thick with fog that makes me cough and kick, or throw up. I hear a woman crying. I hear words: boat trip and rough. I feel terribly, terribly sick. After a very long time, the rocking stops.

A sense of stability settles in. I can smell aromas that are comforting. I hear her chew, then I taste the food. It is as if each mouthful of Eastern European home cooking were on a loudspeaker. Followed by liq-

uids, glug-glug-glug, down her throat and flowing
through her body, and then mine, making the little
bubbles in my ears pop. She sighs, she relaxes.

Then, as I float in my warm sac lolled into utter satisfaction, I discover the one thing I will always adore
about her: she plays the piano.

Chopin, Liszt, Scriabin. Lovely. I particularly enjoy
the Bach Partitas, and let her know by releasing a
healthy burp followed by a stretch. While she plays, we
are both at peace.

In the next part of the dream, I am laughing and
playing with my toes. The woman smiles, kisses my
belly, and grabs my naked, pudgy feet with one cool,
dry hand. I am three months old. Oops! There she
goes; I feel the cold air against my bottom as she pulls
away the damp, messy diaper. Ah, the caress of a warm,
soft washcloth across the belly, down the inside of
moist chubby thighs. Then I'm up again, my full weight
in my shoulders, as the warm cloth delves deep between my cheeks.

I am thinking that I'd rather be in my crib kicking
my feet up in the air, or following the shapes moving
on the mobile. Or compulsively pressing one of the
tune-playing cuddly toys on my bed, and laughing at
the sound of the music, than having to endure her
endless washing.

"Stinky," she says, and wrinkles her nose.

I am lying on the changing table. I don't like what

she's doing. I start to fuss. Ouch! She's got this thing about rubbing my anus with that cloth.

Ouch! Ouch, ouch, ouch! I'm crying now. Crying and kicking and getting very red in the face, sweating and throwing my arms and legs around and making a terrible fuss. Stop it! I don't like it when you do that!

"OK, OK, little one, we're almost done," she says, and starts rubbing lotion on the insides of my thighs.

"Don't cry, little one. I can't handle it when you cry. Don't cry!" she screams.

Does she have any idea how scary she is when she yells? Her face gets all hard, she presses her lips together, and her eyes get big and look as if she's going to fling me against the wall if I don't shut up. I have the right to tell her what I don't like!

"Shut up! Shut up! Shut up! I can't bear to hear you cry!" she shrieks. She puts her hands over her ears and stamps her feet.

I am lying on the changing table naked and cold. Please, cover me up! Hold me. Don't scream at me! Rock me! Feed me! Comfort me! Please stop screaming, screaming, screaming!

I am rocking back and forth and kicking and giving my lungs a good workout when suddenly, oh my. She's covered her fingers in Vaseline and is rubbing it into my thighs. She starts rubbing in the place I pee from.

It feels pretty good. OK. OK. OK. I can get used to this. I'm still cold, but I'm starting to relax. Her fingers continue to slide in and out, rubbing me, gently, pleasurably. I stop crying. I open my eyes and look up at her.

She is laughing and smiling. "That's a good little girl," she says, and slides a dry diaper under my bottom. "Now, Mommy hopes she'll be able to close these damn silly pins before your father gets home."

I awake with a start. I sit up in bed and stare out into the blackness.

I can still feel my body bathed in pleasure, can still feel her smile. I am fighting with myself. This can't be. Am I losing my mind? Why does it feel as if my body remembers? Oh, she couldn't have. Then, within seconds, I am drowning in a tidal wave of knowing and disgust. My body shakes, and I vomit.

Letter to Bette

Hotel La Bella Fortuna
Trieste, California
Land of la bonne grape
July 4, 1973

Ma bete, Bette,

Happy Fourth of July! Are you Independent?
I received the slides of your work this afternoon.
The images are startling, disturbing, and most won-
drous! What an extraordinarily creative obsession to
have developed abroad. Tell me, is it the hashish?

In your last letter you described going to the souk
in the Old City to eat hummus made by an Arab wearing a fez. Are the young Arab boys all gay and lovely?
Will they pose for you before you return to the states? I
would so love to see a photograph of two beautiful
Arab boys wearing eye makeup, girls' clothes, and jewelry, entwined. Somehow, their image seems to be absent, and stands out like a missing persons report.

I've passed the slides around to everyone who is
anyone, and I must say, we are all impressed. I've included in this letter photographs of my red-on-red
paintings. I'm dying to know what you think.

Now I'm sewing pieces of red silk and velvet together to make an opera coat of sorts, a cloak/cape/coat
in various shades of red. When I wear it, I envision my-

self a flame moving from room to room, burning everything in sight with my magnificence.

Have I mentioned that the other thing that has started to fascinate me is Kabuki theatre? I've sent away to Japan for books on kabuki makeup and costumes. I think I'll start a Kabuki theatre here at the hotel and we'll all study Japanese, and the cook will prepare sushi and sukiyaki and green tea.

I'm desperate for someone who can perform a tea ceremony. Do you know of anyone?

I'm learning to meditate. There is a Zen master who visits the hotel once a week and teaches us all breathing and meditation techniques. He's quite interesting. His head is shaved, and he wears dramatic black robes and talks in a softly controlled and reserved way. He seems kind and has a generosity of spirit I find terribly attractive.

At times we chant prior to slipping into meditation. During my most recent meditation, I saw a city on fire. I think it was New York. It was clear to me that it was an atomic holocaust, and all the rooftops were ablaze, and there was red and orange fire reflected in the remaining glass of the buildings.

I immediately ran to tell my Zen teacher. He said that, on the one hand, it might be the mind playing tricks on me, distracting me with pyrotechnics, and on the other, I may have seen something in the future.

Only time will tell which it is.

I can't explain it, but I think I've seen something that is going to happen. Only, I'm afraid that if I tell Mom and Dad they'll say I'm crazy. So please don't tell them, OK? It will stay between us. Just promise me you won't go back to live in New York City, OK?

When are you coming to visit? Your time in Israel should be almost up. I won't be able to visit you. I'm far too busy here, and besides, the whole Middle East/Jewish thing depresses me. So I'll wait for you to come here, to the land of the endless wave, sunsets, and surfers.

Ich liebe und kusse dich,
Lizzie von Liebesweld

Illusion of Memory

Chapter 13

Diary Entry

Jerusalem
July 6, 1973

Since the dream, my desire to paint, or draw, or take pictures has disappeared. Remaining in bed for three days, I have refused all phone calls. Shutters closed, I go over my life in my head. I have been living in some sort of dream. I don't know how else to describe it. Now, the smallest details, like the miniscule roses around the rim of a cup, or the aroma of bergamot tea, unleash long-forgotten memories.

Regardless of the season, my father's morning tea had to be burning hot, even in the dead heat of summer. The morning our neighbor's son was taken to the hospital after falling headfirst off the fire escape onto the tarred roof of the garage four stories down, my father was telling my grandmother that the temperature of his tea was not hot enough.

The boy's mother had been on the phone with a girlfriend instead of keeping an eye on her son, who clambered up and down the fire escape, as he had been doing for weeks. My grandmother had been saying it was a wonder he hadn't killed himself.

His mother was heard laughing one moment, then screaming hysterically the next. When I ran to look out the window, little Chris was lying on the roof like a rag doll, his arms and legs broken.

All week the temperature had been in the high nineties. Luckily, we owned two air conditioners. One was installed in my parents' bedroom and one was placed in the living room. Unable to sleep, I moved from my sweat-rumpled bed to the cool itchiness of the wool carpet on the living room floor, where the air was very cold.

Mom and Dad slept in their bedroom with the door closed. The dog went wherever I did. The short-haired terrier brought to America by my mother was supposed to be her pet. But after my birth, the dog became my bodyguard. Anyone wanting to see me or touch me had to pass muster with the terrier, Pinchie, first.

Pinchie had to be locked in the kitchen whenever the doctor who limped came to examine me. I did not like him, so she bit him. The doctor and my mother communicated in German. One afternoon, he explained how he'd been shot in the leg while escaping a moving train taking all the passengers to Auschwitz. Ever since then, whenever the limping doctor made a house call, my protector Pinchie had to be locked in the kitchen where she barked unabated until he departed.

I don't remember when Mom and Dad started sleeping in separate beds, while still sleeping in the same room. Mom said it was because Dad snored and kept her up. Dad's snoring thundered through the walls to every room. Nevertheless, Mom slept in the queen sized bed in the middle of the room while Dad was forced to sleep in a single bed beneath the window with the air conditioner.

The afternoon after the neighbor's son's death, Grandma was in the kitchen when I returned from the playground. Mom called me into her bedroom. She was lying on Daddy's little bed, naked. The air conditioner was on, and she was letting the cool air blow on her. She told me to close the door behind me, not to let the cool air out.

The room was very quiet except for the hum of the air conditioner.

Mom was lying on her back, her bent legs in the air. They were apart and she had a pearl necklace covering the hairy triangle. I stood looking at her for a few moments. She didn't say anything and I couldn't figure out what she wanted. Then she said, "Look, Betty!" and turned her body around, showing me the pearls gathered between her legs. She let them fall and started to laugh. Then she started pulling them slowly between her hairy lips. She grabbed the clasp between her thumb and index finger and proceeded to unwind the pearls. Gradually she snaked them up her belly to her breasts, where she roped them first around one nipple, and then the other. Her head was thrown back off the edge of the bed and she was laughing and flashing her teeth.

The dog started barking outside the door.

"What's the matter, honey?" she said, laughing hysterically.

I had a funny feeling in my groin, like the way I feel when I've climbed up too high and look down. I ran out of the room, slamming the door behind me, and headed straight into the kitchen for my grandmother, where I hid behind her, clutching her skirt, Pinchie right behind me.

"Where are you going?" Mom shouted from behind the closed door. "Don't you want to play?" Followed by peals of laughter.

I clung to my grandmother's apron and hid my face.

"Was macht sie?" (What is she doing?)

I buried my head deeper in her apron and refused to speak.

Diary Entry

Jerusalem
July 15, 1973

Images cascade across sleep and wakefulness, pictures surging out of my eyes into space. Over my first cup of morning coffee, I sat with Marion Cohn, my best childhood friend who lived up the street. She sat across the table eating a crusty piece of rye bread with a thick slab of sweet butter and asked me for more hot tea. Since childhood, Marion drank tea like a Pole. Always in a glass, never in a cup. I was afraid the glass would break from the heat of the boiling water, but she assured me that she had taken it with her from her mother's house, where all the glass was actually Pyrex.

"Marion has just arrived from Bolivia with her family and only speaks German. You speak German, don't you?" the kindergarten teacher standing by her side had said.

"Yes."

"Good. Then, you will be her translator."

I was four years old and it was the second day of kindergarten. Being a translator had become the norm. I learned English from the neighbor's kids, three-year-old Lenny and his older brother, five-year-old Bobby. Bobby liked me to watch him pee in the bushes. Sometimes, he'd ask me to hold his penis while he did it.

Whenever their mother came to the door needing to talk to my grandmother, or borrow a cup of milk or some sugar, I would translate from English into German. Then I'd translate my grandmother's response into English. And so it would go, back and forth, until the communication was complete.

"Sure," I said authoritatively. "You can leave her with me."

Marion was small, with shiny, red apple cheeks, a turned-up nose, full lips, and chin-length warm brown hair. She wore colorful clothes made out of Bolivian Indian fabrics. I grabbed her hand, told her my name, and in German I told her not to worry, and for the next eight-years, except for the summers when I was sent to sleepaway camp, we were inseparable.

We lived across the street from each other and quickly developed a routine. Each day after school, either I would go to Marion's house, or she would come to mine. We would be given a snack of crusty rye bread with sweet butter, accompanied by a glass of cold milk. At my house, the snack was served by my German-speaking grandmother, while at her house it was served by her German-speaking mother. Snack time was actually an interrogation with food, complete with bright overhead lights.

We'd be asked what we had learned that day, and between mouthfuls of bread, we were expected to articulate, in great detail, what we had studied and how our tests and reports had gone. Only after the questioning had been completed to the satisfaction of the inquisitors, and it was determined we had performed above and beyond expectations, and in turn, nothing terrible had been done to us, were we permitted to go to the bedroom to play "make-believe."

Make-believe was invariably an original script/improvisation, a dramatically imagined and enacted episode of Bonanza, a popular nighttime Western television program. At times, we would take turns playing the regular characters on the show. Other times we'd pretend to be damsels in distress, rescued "just in the nick of time" by Little Joe Cartwright or his swarthy brother, Adam. When playtime was over, we'd return to our respective homes for an hour of piano practice, dinner, and finally homework.

We each had only one surviving grandparent who, along with both parents, had survived the war. At that time, a label for Jews who had survived the camps did not exist. You just saw the tattooed numbers on their arms and knew that whatever they had been through, they did not want to discuss it. They had a tendency toward hysteria, which could be triggered by the most insignificant things. The unexpected news of a friend dying or the discovery of eggs burning in a frying pan often induced similar, if not identical, larger-than-life reactions.

One particularly rainy afternoon, Marion's white-haired grandmother picked us up from school and brought us home, to her house, where we could hardly wait to complete the interactive snack phase and continue where we had left off in our make-believe game the afternoon before. We were just getting to the most important scene of the day, when our play was interrupted.

The bedroom door flew open, banging hard against the wall.

"I want this door open at all times! You have no business closing a door in my house!"

Marion's mother was standing in the hallway, and despite the chill in the air, she was wearing a scanty housedress with nothing underneath, high-heeled slippers, and rubber gloves. She was holding Marion's wet older brother Arnold by the arm, and her long wavy hair, usually up in a French knot, was wild and unkempt. She was screaming at him in English, "You tracked mud into the bathroom!"

We stood motionless. Then Marion's mother started beating Arnold in the face with the heel of her shoe.

"I just finished washing the bathroom floor, and you bring in your dirty boots and mess it up?"

She was hitting him in the face, beating his back, striking him in the head. His hands made a cage around his face, and he was yelling and crying, "You always tell us to put our wet shoes in the bathroom when it rains!"

"Not after I've washed it, you idiot!"

She grabbed him by the back of the neck and continued beating his back and arms with her heel. He pried himself free of her grasp and took off down the hall. She leapt after him, hobbling, shoe raised high in the air, the dark and rather long hair under her arm a dark spot in a white field of flesh.

At that point, Marion's grandmother snuck into the room like a ghost. She sat noiselessly on the bed with her hands folded on her lap, her long silver hair neatly braided around her head like a Christmas wreath, a pale gray woolen shawl draped around her frail shoulders, the fringes falling like tinsel.

"*Sie ist nicht das selbe seit Auschwitz.*" (She has not been the same since Auschwitz.)

We sat down next to her on the bed, as if by being close, we'd somehow be protected. No one spoke. Arnold ran out of the house, barefoot and without a coat, slamming the door behind him. When Marion's mother locked herself in her bedroom, and after we heard the lock turn, her grandmother reached behind her and handed me my coat. I put it on as quietly as I could, tiptoed out the front door, and ran home in the rain, racing along the one long block to our apartment without once looking back.

Before I left for Israel, I went to visit Marion at her family's new apartment two blocks farther up on the avenue, where she and her mother and I sat around the kitchen table of our childhood, speculating about the future and discussing my upcoming move. I found myself staring at the tattooed numerals on Mrs. Cohn's arm. She caught me looking, I froze, and for an instant our eyes met.

Eventually, when Marion went to the bathroom, her mother stood up to put more water in the kettle for tea.

"I once slept with a German soldier for a loaf of bread," she said, her back to me. The copper kettle hit the stove with the weight of the water behind it, and I heard the gas ignite the flame. She turned around and slid seductively into the seat beside me, her elbow touching mine on the cold Formica tabletop.

"I was hungry," she said, very close now. "There was no food. You had to do whatever you could to survive."

She lit a cigarette, took a deep drag, and released a guttural laugh, the smoke coming out of her nostrils.

"I was in the Warsaw Ghetto. I was young. We were starving. You'd do whatever you had to do to stay alive under such circumstances."

She paused and looked into my eyes. I could feel her breath on my eyelashes.

"And if I remember correctly," she said, taking another drag of her cigarette and then tapping the ash into the crystal ashtray, "he was handsome."

Chapter 14

Diary Entry

Jerusalem
July 30, 1973

My upstairs, half-American neighbor, Shoshana, had heard about a remarkable Yemenite palm reader that everyone we knew was raving about. In an effort to lure me out of the house, she went ahead and, without my knowledge, made appointments for us both. It was actually to her credit that she came up with something different with which to entice me. So last night after dinner, we went to the palm reader's rather large apartment in a very bourgeois section of Jerusalem.

Somehow, the setting was not what I had expected. Shoshana insisted on going first while I sat in the plush, modern living room, examining the beige swirling pattern in the white marble floor from my vantage point on the white velvet sofa. I was illuminated by an arched chrome floor lamp which left the rest of the room in relative darkness. I closed my eyes and tried to get in the mood.

Shoshana emerged from the back bedroom precisely forty-five shrink minutes later, in such utter awe that she had to light a cigarette to calm her nerves.

After plunking down on the white velvet plush, she said, "Wow, that was heavy."

Those were the only words she could throw together on such short notice to describe her experience, with simultaneous smoke emerging from every orifice. I took that as my cue and headed, somewhat skeptically, into the back room where the divinations took place.

The palm reader's name was Irit. She was tall, elegant, thin, and very dark. She looked more like an African princess than a middle-class Israeli housewife. Everything about her was long and thin. Her hair, which was swept up high in a ponytail, complemented her intelligent forehead and delicate, even features. Her almond-shaped brown eyes were rimmed in kohl, and beneath each eye was a black dot not unlike the kind the Berber women wore. From her small ears hung long silver and turquoise earrings, and each wrist was adorned with wide silver bracelets made in the filigree Yemenite style. Her lithe body was concealed in a loose-fitting blue-and-white Indian print sheath that went to the floor.

She invited me to sit down and pointed to a gilt Louis XV-style zebra-skin-covered chair. Lit candles stood around the room on tabletops and in windows. Facing the zebra chair was what looked like a throne.

"The chair belonged to a furniture guild in London in the seventeenth century," she said, following my eyes.

"I saw it at a market and couldn't resist it. A kind of madness. It cost more to ship than to buy."

I smiled and sat down. I could feel the zebra skin bristle through my jeans, feeling prickly against the bottom of my thighs. Irit sat and extended her smooth left hand, palm upward, toward me.

"Give me your hand." She followed my lifeline with the index finger of her right hand, checked the flexibility of my thumb, and squeezed the mound. "Are you planning to travel?" she asked in perfect English.

That was almost too funny. A classic moment.

"Yes, I've got a ticket to New York in two weeks."

She looked up from my palm directly into my eyes. "You are certain?"

"Yes."

"You must promise me you will leave."

If this was part of her act, she was starting to make me nervous.

"Why, am I in danger?"

"If you stay, you will be in great danger."

Somehow, this wasn't the way I thought things would go.

"Why?"

"Promise me you will go?"

"Yes, I'm booked."

"Good." She seemed relieved. She smiled and continued the reading. "You are very creative, but you have no luck with men. Although men like you very much, you will only find your true love and your true profession very late in life."

My heart started beating faster, and I noticed that sweat was running from behind my knees.

"What do I do until then?"

"Anything you like. You will travel a great deal. And you will have to overcome a great illness. But that is not for a while."

"Aren't you supposed to tell people only the good things?"

"The illness will change your life for the better."

"Give me some good news, will you?"

"You will have a very long life. But you have a difficult hand, and a difficult life. It will, however, get better as you age. You will have a good old age."

I withdrew my palm. I couldn't believe I had agreed to pay for this.

"That's enough," I said. "I'd like the rest to be revealed in its own good time."

Her dark eyes bore into mine.

"As you wish. There are, however, some things I'd like to reveal to you."

"Thanks, you've already revealed enough."

"There is no need to fear your destiny."

"You don't say?"

I stood up and handed her the money which had been growing warm in my back pocket. I couldn't believe what she did next. She took it and placed it in her bra. She was starting to be a cliché. Then, turning on her heel, Irit escorted me into the living room where my neighbor was sitting shrouded in a cloud of cigarette smoke.

Upon seeing me, she jumped up, the smoke dispersing around her. "How was it?" she chirped.

"Let's go," I answered.

The fortune teller said her good-byes somewhat laboriously, and we exited into the cool Jerusalem night, our sandals making slapping noises against our naked heels as we walked on the stone pavement.

"What happened in there?" she said. "You look terrible."

"She told me to get out of town, that I was in danger if I stayed, and then she went on to say that I would have a long and arduous life filled with illness, loneliness, and misery."

"What?"

"Got any heroin at home? I just might call it quits tonight. What a jerk."

"I can't believe she said that."

"Well, believe it."

As much as I might have wished for an escape, a diversion from dreams and memories did not seem possible.

Diary Entry

The flight to NYC
September 16, 1973

Walking up the steps to the cabin of the El Al 747 headed for New York, I stopped when I reached the top and turned around for one last look.

"Lady, hurry up, will ya?" a man at the end of the line shouted. "We don't got all day."

"You'll be sitting on your fat ass for the next ten hours," I blurted out, "so what's the goddamned rush?"

Some of the passengers standing behind me laughed; others looked away in embarrassment. I allowed my eyes to slowly take in the horizon, while I inhaled one final breath of Middle Eastern air, and moving my tongue back and forth against the roof of my mouth, I luxuriated in its flavor for the last time. Releasing a sigh of inexpressible sadness, I turned and stepped inside. The plane reeked of stale cigarettes, burnt coffee, and Israeli jasmine soap.

The unmistakable smell of jasmine on a breeze of eucalyptus; oh, how I would miss the Hamm Am of the Old City, the Turkish baths. The Hamm Am, as they are called in Arabic and Hebrew, were several cavernous stone rooms hidden inside old buildings in obscure neighborhoods far from the public eye. Within them, steam baths sat alongside saunas. Two stone mikvot were sunk in the ground; ten-foot-by-ten-foot stone pools filled with lukewarm bubbling spring water. The baths were designated for ritual cleansing; religious women were required to submerge themselves after their menses each month.

In another lone room, squares of daylight shot through two overhead stained-glass skylights, casting patches of red, green, and blue shimmering triangles onto the buoyant mineral water of the ice-cold swimming pool that was meant to be taken after the sauna.

Two days out of the week, women were permitted to use the Hamm Am. The rest of the time, the baths were reserved for men. Women, in all shapes and sizes, from every neighborhood in the city and from all over the world, showered and bathed in these communal rooms. The soaping of hair and shaving of limbs was done in full view. Grandmothers initiated grandchildren.

Because it was the tallest building on the block, there was nude sunbathing on the roof. When the women were done browning themselves, it was on to sweating, then cooling and washing.

At the end of the ritual, there was a special room in which to regain one's strength; a square room, with small stained-glass windows east, west, north, and south. Beneath them, striped silk couches lined the walls, and women lay like odalisques, wrapped in sumptuous bath towels, full lips perched on the rims of icy drinks, arms and legs akimbo. Big and fat, small and skinny, it didn't matter. The female form lay about, luxuriating in the sensuality of its femininity, intoxicated by the corporeal's very existence.

The women rested, inhaling the dried eucalyptus and jasmine flowers from the Old City, occasionally stroking their own smooth, cool skin or brushing one another's thick, wavy hair, like lionesses, bedazzling one another with their magnificence.

Some long-hidden part of me had awakened in those baths, and for the first time in my life, I felt whole. I had spent the last weeks removing my paintings from their stretchers and carefully wrapping them around cardboard poles, wide enough for the paint and shellac with which I had coated the images not to crack. I then placed them in larger tubes, sealing and tying the tubes together. The Hamm Am was where I went to unwind, and to reconnect and to prepare for an anxious return with a newfound memory and a dying mother. My visits would be sorely missed.

A little less than an hour ago, I had been discussing whether or not to place the paintings on the conveyor belt that took them to the hold of the plane. When the woman at the check-in counter said that no one would be seated next to me, I decided to bring them along. They stood beside me like my children. Happily seated by the window, I grabbed pillows and blankets from the overhead compartment and settled in for a good snooze.

However, within moments, a handsome young Israeli wearing a white short-sleeved shirt and black slacks, carrying an oxblood leather attaché case handcuffed to his right wrist, with a matching leather belt and sandals, walked determinedly down the aisle and asked to sit, quite deliberately, in the seat next to mine. He offered to move the paintings to the center aisle, and then sat in the seat beside mine.

We talked politely and dined together. He asked endless questions about my family history and what had brought me to Israel. When I asked him about his own life, his responses were curt.

Eventually, we agreed to try to sleep. I stretched out across the two seats by the window, and he lay down in the middle aisle. Trying to sleep was difficult. The drone of the engines kept me awake. Still, I kept my eyes closed and tried to imagine what my homecoming would be like.

Believing I was asleep, he leaned over and frisked me using his left hand.

At first I thought he was trying to feel me up, but no, he was looking for something. I pretended not to notice. When he wasn't looking, I opened my eyes and saw that the attaché case had been disconnected from his right wrist.

We arrived in New York on time, and as I trundled off to take my baggage, out of the corner of my eye I could see him and his attaché case, now reattached to his wrist, disappear behind customs.

PART TWO

New York

My skin quit registering the various changes in the breeze, and smells seemed to have faded from the world entirely, my nose waking up only once or twice a day, perhaps while cooking, or when taking out the garbage.

—*David Abram*

Chapter 15

Diary Entry

New York City
September 26, 1973

Jewish New Year is tomorrow. Mom has locked herself in her bedroom for the past two days and refuses to come out. Grandma has secluded herself in her upstairs apartment and declines all invitations to visit. If I want to see her, I have to go upstairs. Sylvia has been denied entrée to our home. Dad disappears to the office every morning at 6:00 a.m., and returns in the evening after dinner. I feel as if I'm living in a madhouse. I haven't got the faintest idea what is going on, and everyone denies that there is anything wrong. I have no idea why they were so insistent that I return from Jerusalem. No one has talked to me since my arrival. I can't imagine what Rosh Hashahna will be like.

I called Pratt Institute this morning regarding my exhibition. In my absence, there appears to have been a fire in the main building where all the records were kept; they have no idea who I am. It would follow, they have no proof of my upcoming exhibition.

If only I had known these things beforehand. I would have stayed in Israel. I was offered an exhibition at Gidon's Gallery in Jerusalem, the hottest new gallery in town. I turned it down because I believed I was coming home to a one-woman show of my work at the Pratt Institute's gallery in New York. I'll simply have to dig up my old paperwork and prove to them that I exist, and that they owe me an exhibition. I don't understand why they didn't say anything when I contacted them from Israel. Well, now we'll see whether they make good on their promise.

If not, I'll simply contact Gidon and return to Jerusalem.

Chapter 16

Letter to Lizzie
New York City
September 26, 1973

Dearest Lizzie,

Last night, I celebrated Rosh Hashahna with Leslie and her brother.

We went to her parents' place on Beekman Place. It was fun, and the dogs were everywhere, and her father smoked a big fat cigar after the meal. When her parents retired to their bedroom to watch TV, we decided to go downtown to Little Italy for the San Genaro festival, where I saw a teenager lying in a pool of blood.

Moments earlier the boy had been standing. He drove his hands deep into his jacket pockets as he watched an older man in cowboy boots and sunglasses approach.

From where I stood, I could see that the boy had slipped his fingers into a set of steel knuckles off which a spark of light reflected. Even though the kid didn't say a word, his attitude was cocky. He was certain he would knock out his opponent. Maybe even break the stocky, tough-looking adversary's jaw.

His rival wore an old motorcycle jacket and stood

utterly still. Then, with one swift yet gentle motion, he caressed the younger man's throat with a razor concealed in his palm. The gesture was so tender, so filled with sorrow, that the young man could not comprehend what had happened. Using the fingers of his left hand, he touched the wetness at his throat. Then he looked up in disbelief, his long black eyelashes fluttering briefly prior to his legs collapsing beneath him. The man in the motorcycle jacket snapped the razor shut without wiping it, then turned on his cowboy boot heels and disappeared into the crowd.

I sat beside the body for some time watching the blood from the gash in his neck flow down the grate into the sewer. I was shaking so hard that I barely felt the pair of beefy hands grab both my shoulders while a man's voice whispered in my ear, "Don't touch him. You don't know who he belongs to."

Then the pair of hands lifted me up and gently pushed me into the moving crowd. I was immersed in moving bodies and garish carnival lights, enveloped in the thick, sweet smell of zepole, and the sizzle of sausages, peppers, and onions, afloat in a sea of damp wool, sweat, and acrid, stained underwear. I stumbled for a while in a haze, needing to vomit.

Out of the blue, there was the harsh sting of a hand grabbing my ass. I seized the hand and turned to look into the face. He had the shortest crew cut of sandy hair I'd ever seen. His eyes were blue and beady and he was laughing. He had exceptionally full lips and there was dried spittle in the corners of his mouth. The garish lights emphasized his pasty skin, which was red and greasy from alcohol. The blue and green bulbs reflected off his shiny face which he put close to mine. I could smell the onions and beer on his breath as he spoke.

"I've always had a thing for blondes."

I slapped him across the face and kneed him in the balls as hard as I could. Then I screamed, "What did you say?"

He was on his knees with his hands cupping his balls, cursing me. I threw myself into the crowd as fast as I could. Where the hell were my friends? Just when I needed them most, they had disappeared.

I kept moving and the streets became emptier. I ran from one corner to the next, the frigid, dirt-laden wind pounding at my face. Off in the distance, I saw a bus waiting at the stop and rushed on. Sitting back, the light's white glare washed over me. The seat felt icy through my jeans. I was no longer used to the cold. Teeth chattering, I crossed my legs to stay warm. The heat was like a heckler, jeering the few late-night passengers between stops. I breathed deeply, and realized that I was saturated in my own sweat. I can't bear it here. I dream of returning to Jerusalem. My exhibition of paintings and photographs that was scheduled for a mid-November opening in the Graduate Gallery has been cancelled. Meanwhile, not all the painted pieces have arrived. I'm so tempted to go back and accept the show I was offered in Jerusalem.

This week, when I unwrapped the work that did arrive and spread it out around the living room for Dad to see, he slowly examined each piece, then turned to me and said, "For this, I sent you to Israel?" Then he turned around and walked away, shaking his head.

He and I are supposed to go to the Modern to see the new Picasso exhibition this weekend. At least that is neutral territory, and we'll be able to argue good-naturedly about which pieces we like best, and why.

Please write to me soon. I'm at my wits' end.

> Love,
> XOXOXOXOXOXO
> Ta Bête, Bette

Diary Entry

NYC
October 6, 1973

It is Yom Kippur. Israel was attacked last night by the Egyptian Army and has suffered enormous casualties. I've been on the phone trying to reach Amos in Jerusalem and his father in Beersheba, but no matter what time I've phoned, no one has answered.

When I am not on the phone, I'm glued to the TV. I feel helpless and frightened. I've contacted the Jewish Agency on Park Avenue. They say they need volunteers to man the phones and canvass for medical supplies. They need money. I want to go back to Israel, but all flights in and out of the country are cancelled. The Jewish Agency said to come; we need you.

Chapter 17

Diary Entry

New York City
October 8, 1973

The war in Israel continues. I know only what I hear on the news and what I overhear at the Jewish Agency. Still no news from Amos.

Meanwhile, at home I'm in a time warp.

I am sitting naked on one of the two matching white silk Bergere chairs in the living room that face a wall of windows onto the street. The chairs have always reminded me of Marie Antoinette, plump breasts falling out of brocade bodices, powdered wigs that look like stacked wedding cakes sitting atop white face powder and vermilion-colored lips, a mouche seductively displayed in the corner above the upper lip. Two French courtesans seduce me in my parents' living room, the living room in which I sat as a child.

Mom has finally emerged from the bedroom and has gone to the hairdresser, and Dad is, as per usual, at the office. He gets there early, so that he can work until very late undisturbed. No one hears him leave. The living room has retained its museum quality: everything in its place, down pillows plumped to perfection, the paintings and prints my father has spent a lifetime acquiring beautifully framed and hung.

There is a new sculpture. A nineteenth-century bronze archer—Apollo, no doubt—drawing a bow while he steps forward gingerly, chin high, nose turned upward. I check the signature: Max Oschmann, German, a fairly obscure turn-of-the-century artist from Berlin. This inability to separate from them is most annoying. They kill us, and we continue to buy their cars, admire and collect their artists, read their books, and listen to their music.

Leonard Bernstein was recently touted as a genius for his interpretation of Mahler's Fifth; we seek an inexplicable merging through art. My father is named after Siegfried of Siegfried and Isolde. His mother was, after all, an opera singer.

My parents' taste is Bauhaus. A Mies van der Rohe Barcelona table stands over an Oriental rug. On the other side of the room sits a Le Corbusier pony skin chaise lounge, ultramodern furniture mixed chicly with the occasional French antique; the unconscious balance of masculine and feminine, pure functionality sidling up to the frivolous.

Like the furniture, my parents have grown closer to each other in my absence. They are actually civil to each other. He spoils her. Defers to her. What can he do? She is dying. A life stands in the wings waiting to depart. Do they love each other as they sleep in separate beds? She is depressed. Locks herself in her room and shuts the door, not emerging for days on end.

Yesterday, I hid her slippers, the ones with the ostrich feathers at the toe, in the freezer. I checked on them in the afternoon, and the feathers were crunchy. She looked all over the house. First she cursed herself. Then she cursed me.

"You've taken them!" she said.

"No, I haven't seen them. Really," I responded.

And finally, only after she had given up, and decided to prepare dinner, how surprised she was. There behind the freezer door, instead of bread ready for the oven, were her pink slippers with the icy feathers. As I sat in the living room, I heard her guffaw, a belly laugh that made her breast scar ache. And for that one moment she forgot that she was dying.

We went for a walk in the park on Sunday. The sun was warm and we walked slowly. She put her arm through mine. Physical contact with her has always made my skin crawl. As long as I can remember, it has been that way. I want to run, to tell her that she leans too heavily upon me; that after a lifetime of leaning, the clown is tired. The clown wants her own life.

But instead, I crack a joke.

When she smiles, exposing her yellowing, cancer-ridden teeth, framed in the decaying skin which hangs off her bones like a sagging dress with brown spots, and her once shiny and glamorous hair crackles to the soft finger's touch, so dry and brittle, I can see in her eyes that she wants to die. She wants the kind of peace that only death can provide.

"You've lost too much weight in Israel," she says. "You should be more careful, or soon, no man will want to look at you."

It's always too much or too little. I am too fat or too slim. Never right.

"I want to talk about your sister Sylvia," I say.

"There is nothing to discuss," she says. "She's crazy, and that's all there is to it."

"I don't think so," I reply.

"What the hell do you know? You're a nothing."

Delightful, really. What a homecoming. I'm a nothing. You're a somebody, a larger-than-life heroine, the one who survived the most horrendous of the horrendous. You say you did it for me. But I know better. All the previous babies, aborted. All except me. Her logic was quintessentially German. She was saying that there was a hierarchy to consider. And that I was at the bottom.

"She was always a little off, you know," she says, "from the time she was a baby."

Sylvia was a little off, and I'm a nothing.

"It's not enough that I have cancer," she says, looking at me accusingly now, tears gathering in the corners of her eyes, "but I am a bad mother, too? Of course, it's all my fault. When in doubt, blame the mother."

The dream came back to me in a flash. I tore my arm away from hers and stepped away. I was longing to say, "I've remembered."

But I couldn't. We stood looking at each other. I silently wished that the earth had parted so that I could leap into its molten core.

All around us children played and ran, birds chirped and sang, traffic blared, but I heard nothing save the aching of my heart.

Diary Entry

New York City
October 12, 1973

When my mother awoke this morning, she could not swallow. We phoned the doctor, who sent the ambulance to take her to Lenox Hill Hospital. When she was gone, I noticed she had left her engagement ring behind in the ashtray next to her bed; the oval cabochon emerald encased in a yellow gold band, like an egg in a crate, flanked on either side by red gold scrolls, and bound by rows of diamonds. Of all the jewelry she owned, I'd admired that ring most as it sat on my mother's delicate and feminine hand. Perhaps, I appreciated it because I knew, somewhere in the back of my mind, that someday it would be all I would have of her.

The end of WWII marked the beginning of my parents' life as free people. Living on the Turkenstrasse in the artsy section of Munich known as Schwabbing, they spent their time trying to discover which family members were left alive, while attempting to determine where to go next.

My father took off for one year, making a pilgrimage to Kutno, Poland, where his parents had lived. He discovered they had been murdered at Treblinka at about the same time that he, my mother, her sister, and my grandmother had been arrested and imprisoned. They were arrested under the Nazis and continued to be imprisoned under the Russians. After their release, they survived by living on the run under assumed names with matching identity papers created by my father's own hand, as Christian Germans. They lived in constant fear of being recognized and exposed by those who had known them before the war.

When he started to earn money at his new position as a translator at the International Refugee Organization, he secretly purchased two matching cabochon emeralds. He then set about, just as secretly, designing the settings for a ring and matching pendant. He sought out a jeweler to have the two pieces made according to his specifications; they were to be my mother's engagement ring and necklace.

My parents had been living together since 1939 and my mother owed her life to him. Spotting her in a café in Czernovitz, Romania, shortly after his escape from Poland, my father liked to say he'd fallen in love at first sight.

Several days before, on a moonless night in March, he swam the icy Dniester River with a Polish child strapped to his back. Her father had been arrested for being a member of the resistance. The snow on the ground, the wet clothes freezing to his skin and chilling him to the bone, resulted in a lifelong battle with sciatica.

Members of the underground were waiting for them in the woods.

They had to escape while the night was still pitch-black, and lighting a match was forbidden lest a sniper see it and shoot. I've never been able to figure out how they managed to find one another in the dark.

The next day, he appeared with a new identity and a new profession; always a talented artist, he offered his services painting movie posters. It was the ideal cover for his underground activities. Because my father fell in love the moment he saw my mother, to prove his serious intentions, he offered to create false identity papers for her and her family.

To protect Grandmother, who was forty-eight years old at the time, he created documents stating she was insane. That way, if she was arrested and questioned, the Nazis would never really trust her testimony or bother torturing her for information.

The documents stood her in good stead. She was never tortured. By living under false identities, they avoided being trapped in the ghetto and having to wear the identifying yellow star.

As their lives together progressed, my father took numerous moody black-and-white photographs of my mother, shaded in German Expressionist lighting, the inevitable cigarette smoldering seductively in the hand that wore the ring. Legend has it that an envious Nazi neighbor stole the pendant out of my mother's bedroom while she entertained her German guests at the piano during an afternoon party.

As long as I can remember, my mother wore the emerald ring. Like a hazy crystal ball, the emerald was a classical composition of imperfections: cracked, chipped, and cloudy, it was a reflection of her soul, and a forecast of their years to come. But no matter how loudly or how often they fought, in the forty years that they were married, I rarely saw her hand without it.

My mother had an unusual philosophy regarding marriage. "Always have your own money," she'd say repeatedly, "and make sure that he loves you more than you love him. If you have your own money, you can always leave. If he loves you more, he'll never leave you."

A classically trained pianist who practiced every day, each afternoon when I returned from high school, I would hear the sad notes of a Chopin etude wafting down the carpeted hallway before the elevator door had even opened. Sometimes, as I approached our apartment building on East 74th Street, if the windows to the living room had been left open, I would be able to hear the first notes from the street.

After three o'clock, the door was left unlocked. At times she simply left it ajar; a heavy metal door resting on an open lock. I would enter and quietly put my books down on the floor while she continued to play. In the cobalt blue and gold ashtray that sat next to the note stand on the baby grand Chickering piano, deep

inside its bowl would be her rings, the green emerald
barely concealing the thinly etched rose gold wedding
band lying beneath it.

We would not speak. I would simply enter the
room, hang up my coat, and after removing my shoes,
stretch out on the down-filled, sea-foam green velvet
sofa, where I would close my eyes and start to drift in
and out of the music, accompanied by the faint click of
her nails against the ivory keys, and the muffled sound
of her slipper-clad foot on the piano's brass pedals.
Then, when she had played to her heart's content, she
would stop. And we two would sit in the ensuing silence, car horns faintly drifting up from the street
below, the light of the room slowly growing dim.

Chapter 18

Diary Entry

New York City
October 24, 1973

The phone rang at 3:00 a.m. Sylvia's acquired Hungarian accent summoned me to the hospital. When I arrived, Mom was surrounded by doctors and nurses; they were suctioning the phlegm out of her throat.

The doctor took us aside and said that it would not be long. Dad was sitting in a leather chair, his head limp against his chest.

Sylvia left the room as I entered and walked into the hallway. The woman lying in the bed looked like a shrunken version of my mother. In the brief time she had been in the hospital, her face had become palsied on one side, and she had lost her ability to speak. Her small frame was trembling.

She motioned for me to come closer, motioned for me to hold her. I assured the nurses that it would be OK. Taking my mother's small frame in my arms, I cradled her head in my hands.

"I'm afraid," she mumbled out of one side of her mouth.

"There is nothing to fear," I said. "You can let go."

The words came out as if I were possessed. What

right did I have to tell her not to be afraid?

"Everything is all right," I reassured her. "There is nothing to fear."

How could I say that with such conviction?

She looked into my eyes, fright and panic seeking comfort, her delicate hands lying crossed and limp on her chest. She gasped for breath, and on the second exhale, her soul departed.

Realizing what had happened, my father suddenly got up from his chair and faced the bed, while Sylvia stood in the doorway examining the scene.

"I can't watch," Sylvia said, turning away.

Then she motioned for my father to come with her as she walked into the hospital corridor. He stood immobile, not knowing what to do. Sylvia shouted his name again, only this time it was a command. His head turned downward toward his shoes, he slowly put one foot in front of the other, and walked out of the room to meet her.

Diary Entry

New York City
October 26, 1973

The day of my mother's funeral, the phone rang at
3:30 a.m. Ronit's accented English sounded as if she
were around the corner rather than thousands of miles
away.

"I'm sorry to wake you."

"What has happened?"

Silence.

"You didn't wake me up at three thirty in the
morning to breathe in my ear."

"It's Amos."

"Is he alive?"

"No."

I felt a ripping sensation in my chest.

"When?"

"He stepped on a land mine. Yesterday in the late
afternoon."

Hot tears stung my cheeks.

"Does his father know?" I asked between sobs.

"Yes."

"Ronit? I loved him."

"I know." She paused. "There is more."

I inhaled.

"Gidon," she said.

"Gidon what?"

"We are waiting for the details. He was taken prisoner by the Egyptians."

"What can I do?"

"Nothing, my darling. Pray. I'll let you know as things develop."

"When is Amos's funeral?"

"Don't know yet."

"Call me?"

"Of course."

"I wish I could have told him..."

"He knew."

"How do you know?"

"I know. Shalom."

"Shalom, my friend."

Sitting up in bed, the receiver locked in a cold hand, I felt my soul leave my body and hide in a sealed black metal box. I felt numb. Nothing more might enter, and nothing may exit. Hidden inside alongside my soul is my mother's ring, and a photo of Amos.

Outside the box, my ghost attended my mother's funeral. Her sister, my aunt Sylvia, appeared in a red suit, with matching handbag, stilettos, and ruby-rimmed sunglasses. She even found the time to touch up the roots of her platinum hair. She put her arm through my father's the moment we reached the funeral home, and there it stayed throughout the day.

After the burial, my grandmother took the ghost

aside.

"I have something important to tell you."

"What?"

"You must be careful now."

"Careful?"

"They have been having an affair for years."

"Who?"

"Your father and your aunt."

I stood looking at her in stunned silence.

"Did Mom know about this?"

"You stupid child. Why do you think the sisters did not speak?"

"Ah."

"They are dangerous. They will take everything."

"There is nothing to take."

"There is something, and they will take it."

I felt faint. I sat down. I was offered a cup of strong black coffee with sugar and a cognac, which I accepted. Someone took my pulse and announced it was slow. Another pair of hands stroked my hair and fed me the coffee and cognac.

But the door to the outside world had effectively shut. I watched the ghost stumble a bit upon rising to leave the room and head for her childhood bedroom, where she would remain, lying in the bed in which she had slept as a child. For ten days, she would sleep in the same clothes she had worn to her mother's funeral.

At the end of the ten days, on the morning of the eleventh day, the ghost would overhear Sylvia talking to a doctor. She would hear her tell him that Bette had stopped speaking and eating, that there was something wrong. That she had been silent and unmoving for ten days, and that she, Sylvia, and my father were concerned. The ghost could hear from Sylvia's response that the doctor suggested Bette had been under a great deal of stress, that it was understandable. To give Bette some time. That her mother's death was a great shock. I could hear my father standing next to her, rubbing up against her as he pressed his ear alongside the receiver so that he could listen in on the conversation.

In the end, Sylvia reluctantly conceded. But not before saying something about having a friend who worked at Payne Whitney who would gladly take Bette in. After she hung up, the ghost heard what sounded like a long, wet kiss.

Chapter 19

Diary Entry

NYC
November 5, 1973

The ghost didn't know what else to do. So she waited until everyone had gone out and then phoned Annie Blau. They had gone to high school together, and during those years had been inseparable. Her father, Dr. Paul Blau, was a renowned Jungian therapist.

The ghost explained there was death everywhere and she did not want to speak, that even this small effort was terribly painful. Annie offered to call her father on the ghost's behalf, saying that she'd call back within minutes, which she did.

"He'd be happy to see you," she said. "I'll meet you at my parents' apartment."

Anne had been a childhood actress in NYC. When Bette went off to college to become a visual artist, she became a drama major at Yale. The ghost hadn't been to the apartment on West 85th Street, in which Bette and Annie had played as children, in years. The ghost attempted to recall the last time. Was it the Christmas before Anne starred in The Lion in Winter? That must have been at least three years ago.

Yet, there was such kindness and compassion in

Annie's voice that when she offered to help, the ghost felt like a man dying of thirst in the desert who is suddenly offered a cool glass of water; hands trembling, the ghost accepted.

Wrapping a long purple wool scarf around her neck, she put on a coat. She next considered whether she really wanted to brush her teeth prior to walking through the park, and then decided she didn't. At four o'clock in the afternoon the sky was getting dark. The trees were bare, and the street lamps seemed to be on low. Entering the park at 72nd Street and Fifth Avenue, the wind blew the grit of the city around so that it made circles on the sidewalk.

People were rushing, holding their heads down, urgently clutching their scarves; everyone had somewhere important to go.

The ghost arrived at the fountain off 72nd and Fifth, as if a UFO had picked her up, made her forget the experience, and then beamed her there, not knowing whether the journey was a vague memory or a figment of her imagination.

There had been a time when the precise view before which she now stood had been her favorite. From beside the fountain could be seen the lake, a few bucolic hills and empty trees, and in the distance, the impressive buildings of Central Park West. The ghost lit a cigarette and looked across the pond. As the smoke escaped her nostrils, she imagined bodies smoldering through chimneys. Had the war never happened, might her family have been different? Had the war created them? Had the war created her? From inside the black box, Bette felt safe. No one could touch her.

She felt numb, inside and out. Taking a final drag, she threw down the remaining cigarette butt and, like snuffing out a life, crushed it with the heel of her boot.

As she did so, she berated herself for smoking, and told herself yet again that she should quit. Suddenly, from somewhere deep inside the box, Bette realized that nothing mattered. For all she knew, the following week she might be sitting in a much bigger black box. If it were up to Sylvia, she'd have Bette committed to an asylum.

Diary Entry

NYC
November 6, 1973

Anne was standing in front of the 1920s pre-war smoking a thin cigarette when the ghost spotted her. As waiflike as ever, she wore a miniskirt that showed off her sensational black-clad legs which seemed to start somewhere at her neck and end at her stack-heeled black pumps.

Her pale blonde hair looked freshly highlighted, and she wore it as she always had, blunt cut and parted down the middle, ending sharply at her chin. Her fingernails were manicured with a delicate pale pink translucent polish that made her perfect, long fingers look even longer and more perfect. Bette watched her hand as she brought the elegantly ringed fingers to her freshly glossed lips and inhaled as if it were simply impossible to get enough smoke in just one drag.

Her coat was made of expensive black cashmere, and almost hid her miniskirt, but for a quarter of an inch. On this street, for as long as Bette could remember, the wind had always howled like a bandit off the Hudson River regardless of season, making the walk from one corner to another a physical challenge for young and old alike. With the wind at the ghost's face, she slowed down and for a time stood watching Annie smoke, as if it were the most fascinating thing in the world.

The only bit of color Anne would ever have allowed took the form of a wool scarf wrapped twice around her neck, which at that moment flew up and twisted itself between the strands of her hair, almost burning in a tangle of angelic gold and fiery ash.

Despite the fact that it was already dark, Anne wore enormous sunglasses, over which her pale blue eyes, lined and mascaraed, peered out like periscopes, looking from left to right and then back again. When she saw Bette, she let out a yelp of recognition and came running, those long legs covering great amounts of ground, skinny arms open wide, the cigarette bearing her lip print thrown carelessly to the wind, the fashionable black handbag hanging off her shoulder flapping wildly.

The ghost threw herself into her arms and began to cry.

"It's OK," she said, "everything will be OK. Paul will take care of everything."

It had always struck Bette as odd that Anne referred to her father by his first name, but she assumed that that was something all the children of therapists did, and as she inhaled her perfume mixed with cigarette smoke, Bette broke down, waves of gratitude washing over her.

Annie helped her to the old wooden elevator

which creaked and jostled its way slowly up to the fifth floor. She was taller, and the ghost placed her head on Annie's shoulder as they rode. It was then that the ghost realized that she had developed an uncanny sense of smell. Closing her eyes, she could smell a variety of dinners wafting past them on the stale breeze of the elevator shaft.

Somewhere in the building a tenant had ordered in Chinese, while from an apartment playing opera somewhere on the third floor, a southern Italian spaghetti sauce with meatballs was simmering. As the elevator door opened, it was clear that meatloaf accompanied by roasted potatoes was just minutes away from being served at the Blau residence.

"*Ach*, Bettylein!" said Paul, rising out of his favorite chair. "Please, come in! Come in!"

He looked well, his graying pale brown hair slicked back like a 1940s crooner, tall and thin like Anne, with full lips and a beauty mark in the corner above his mouth that gave the tall German a decidedly feminine twist.

"Harriet vill be zo pleazed to see you! Are you staying for dinner? Ach yah, you must, I insist!"

That settled, the ghost took a seat on the sofa, folded her hands in her lap like a schoolgirl, and crept into herself. There was nothing to do but look around the room. The ghost thought the apartment looked remarkably the same. The piano still stood next to the French doors, the velvet couch still stood against the wall, the white shag carpeting was still white and still shag, and the dining room, which stood off the living room separated by French doors, was still lined in floor-to-ceiling bookcases jammed with books.

Paul and Anne made small talk, while the ghost sat by uncomfortably.

"Bettylein, vood you like to hev our little converzayshon now, rasser zan layter?"

Paul sounded remarkably like Henry Kissinger at that moment. But rather than tell him so, the ghost rose, nodded, and waited for him to lead the way.

"All right, zen, follow me," he said, rising from his favorite chair.

They ended up in the bedroom. His wife had moved into Anne's bedroom since her daughter's departure for school. There had been rumors that he had slept with some of his patients. He sat on the bed and offered her a chair.

"Now, vat seems to be ze trouble?"

The ghost couldn't find her voice at first. Paul waited.

"It is very hard to speak. My mother is dead. My lover is dead. I'm living inside a black box. And my father and aunt are trying to have me committed."

The ghost began to cry.

"Ridiculous!" Paul shouted. "You're just an average

neurotic. You don't need to be locked away." Appreci-
ating his own joke, he laughed. "You are not psychotic.
You didn't sign anything, did you?"

"No"

"Good. Don't! And if zey pressure you, call me."

"I'm so afraid."

He put his hand on her shoulder, looked deep into
her eyes, and said, "You've nasing to fear. I'll recom-
mend zomeone for you to see. Zis not speaking zing,
as charming as it may be, iz not productive. You must
free up vatever iz blocking you, and speak up!"

"Oh, Paul, you don't want to know what is going
on?"

"You're right. I don't. But here's ze name of
somvone who does." Paul scribbled the name, address,
and telephone number on a piece of paper and
handed it to the ghost. "I zink you should see a
woman. Don't you?"

Bette could not respond.

"Take my verd for it, OK? She's great. You'll be fine
in no time! Shell vee eat?" And as he stood up to leave,
his right hand brushed against the ghost's left breast.

"My, how you've grown," he said, and left the
room.

Chapter 20

Diary Entry

NYC
December 1, 1973

The ghost is sitting in the therapist's office, one room in a rambling, elegantly furnished Upper West Side apartment, facing the corner of West 86th Street and Central Park West. The walls are lined with books. There is what appears to be a sandbox on top of a table. There are toy figures in the sandbox.

The therapist is sitting in a chair looking at me. She has curly brownish-red hair that frames her face and falls to her shoulders. She wears glasses. They are rather fashionable, large red frames through which she peers at me from her desk. She is wearing a beige sweater and a matching camelhair skirt, flat brown leather shoes, and stockings, and is sitting in a coordinating beige leather chair with a footstool. The clothes and furniture are understated and of the finest quality.

In another part of the house, an African-American woman with a Southern accent is saying something about not having enough eggs. Followed by the sound of a heavy metal door slamming.

Meanwhile, the therapist and I sit in silence, which is fine with me.

Every so often, she cocks her head slightly to the side like a bird ogling me with one eye. I find it alarming and look away. She clears her throat like an opera singer about to sing her first note and opens her mouth.

"Let's begin?"

The ghost, who is wearing dirty sneakers, jeans, and a sweater, and whose hair has not been washed in two weeks, nods curtly.

"Dr. Blau tells me you've had a shock of some sort. Why don't you tell me about it?"

The ghost turns her head and looks out the window. Then, to her own amazement, she speaks.

"Everyone is dead."

"Who is everyone?"

"Everyone," she says, and continues looking out the window.

The ghost sits in the chair while I crawl deep inside my black box. I am sitting way in the back where no one can reach me.

"Is your mother one of the dead?"

"Yes."

"Who else is with her?"

The ghost closes her eyes, as if by closing them she will be able to see the outline of Amos's face and feel his hands on her body. As if by closing her eyes she will be able to see her flamboyant sister in an open convertible, her wild red hair flying in the wind. The ghost closes her eyes, in order to better see her mother's face, when she was a vibrant young woman. But in its place, the ghost relives her mother's shriveled body taking its last gasp. And from somewhere deep inside, she starts to weep.

The therapist does nothing. We all sit together and cry. She hands the ghost a box of tissues.

"I wish I had a magic wand," the ghost says.

"What would you change?"

The weeping begins again.

"Everything."

"Where would you begin?"

The ghost still cries, but now I know that the therapist isn't terribly bright. Everyone knows that everything that ever was had to begin at the beginning.

"The war."

She peers over the tops of her glasses and slowly repeats my words.

"The war?"

The ghost wonders whether she is hard of hearing.

"Yes. The war."

"Which war?"

"Which war?"

"Yes."

"The second."

"World War Two?"

The ghost considers the remark for a moment.

"Yes, World War Two."

"Do you come from a family of immigrants?"

"Doesn't everyone?"

"Not really."

"Of course they do."

"Let's not quibble."

"I've always liked the word *quibble*."

"Yes, it's an expressive word."

"Why is there a sandbox in your office?"

"So that patients can play in it."

"Like reading tea leaves?"

"Not exactly."

"Please don't tell me it's a science."

"Don't you like science?"

"Science is OK. But tea leaves and sandboxes don't qualify."

"What qualifies?"

"Going to the moon. A cure for cancer. A reason for living."

"Do you ask yourself why you are here?"

"No."

"Did you ever?"

"Maybe."

"Are you in pain?"

"For as long as I can remember."

"Your family wants to have you committed."

"I know."

"I don't think you need to be committed. I'd like

to prevent them from putting you away. Would you work with me twice a week? Can you do that?"

Twice a week seems a minor inconvenience for remaining free.

"I think so."

"Good. Then I'll see you on Tuesdays and Thursdays at four o'clock."

"Four o'clock?" the ghost repeats like a magpie. And she slowly stands up and slips out the door. She slips back in and says,

"I'm sorry. What's your name?"

The therapist cocks an eyebrow and says,

"Call me Roberta."

Roberta's Journal Entry

NYC
December 5, 1973

I've taken on a new client. Her name is Elizabeth, she is twenty-three years old and has stopped communicating to those nearest to her. During our first meeting, she sat silently looking out the window for the first fifteen minutes of the session. Then surprisingly, when I suggested we begin, she actually began to speak. I expected more resistance. She is severely depressed.

For our first meeting, she wore filthy jeans and an old ratty sweater. Her hair was unwashed. When she finally spoke, it was in clipped phrases and hushed tones. She appears to be in a great deal of pain. Dr. Blau was the referring physician, and would only say that both the girl's mother and her lover recently died, within days of each other, sending the patient into severe mourning and a deep depression bordering on catatonia.

At one point, she began to cry, which I took as a very good sign. The crying indicates that she is able to feel. She is not as numb as I first thought. And perhaps not as remote. She must feel terribly lonely.

Elizabeth's father's response to his daughter's loss was expressed in a desire to commit her. Although one assumes he must feel intense grief at the loss of his wife of so many years, and may not be acting out of a stable and loving place, the truth may be otherwise. His motives seem questionable. I believe the patient is feeling a deep sense of betrayal, which she is unable to acknowledge.

Since the death of the mother, the aunt, the mother's sister, has stepped into the mothering role. From our phone conversations, she wants to take control of her niece's future and is supposedly concerned about the girl's well-being. Yet, she has made it clear that she finds the patient incompetent and unmanageable.

However, rather than wait for the patient to regain her bearings, the aunt is eager to deposit the young woman at Payne Whitney. Which could guarantee the end of the girl's freedom forever.

The patient has no one to turn to but me, and so has agreed to enter the therapeutic process twice weekly. That is a good sign. That way, I can keep the family at bay while we begin to bring to light the patient's painful history, culminating in the trauma of the mother's death, and the full reason behind the patient's retreat into her private world.

Dr. Blau, who is my therapist and to whom I report weekly, feels that this case will allow me to flex certain therapeutic muscles that heretofore have remained unexercised. I will be the patient's guide into the unconscious, and Dr. Blau will continue to be mine.

My experience of the young patient is that she is like a knotted ball of thread. One by one, the threads must be extricated and examined. The challenges will be many; not only will they be of a therapeutic nature, but more than likely of the legal variety as well. I hope that I am up to the task. The patient needs someone in her court. Dr. Blau and I will take the place of her parents, and will do our best to nurture and protect her from her own family until she recovers.

Both Dr. Blau and I suspect early childhood violence of both a physical and emotional nature, a combination of neglect and maltreatment resulting in a long-repressed trauma, the unconscious memory of which has been triggered by the death of the mother and lover. Her feelings of exploitation and alienation replicate an earlier response to the unconscious trauma, resulting in disaffection from a family that could not accept her (for whatever imagined reasons). Her silence in the family's presence represents a regression to a preverbal phase, in which she was not held accountable for her actions, or perhaps it is a return to the scene of the initial crime, which took place when she was not yet able to speak, and therefore was unable to "speak up" for herself.

Illusion of Memory

Chapter 21

Diary Entry

NYC
December 20, 1973

This morning from my window, I saw two pigeons smoking cigars. Scruffy, gray, and fat, they sat with very pink feet curled beneath them on top of a small air-conditioning unit that was plugged into a bedroom window on the ground floor of a brownstone across the street, looking like a cork in a bottle. Wrapped around the air conditioner was some gray waterproof material, held on by packing string. And tied to one side, a one-eyed powder blue teddy bear stood guard, small mouth agape, like an urban sadomasochistic scarecrow, bound by several rounds of gaffer's tape.

The two red glowing embers silently sat side by side, like the oldest of friends. I saw neither matches nor a lighter nearby, nor was a lit candle apparent any-where in the vicinity. I stood silently, trying not to breathe lest my presence be felt, when, cigars still in beaks, they flew over to the brand new BMW parked directly in front of my window and, still puffing away, took a shit and began to speak.

"Jack, I tell ya," said one gray bird to the other, "I had the best burger last night at J. G. Mellon's, around the corner."

"Yeah," said the second pigeon, "good beer on tap, too. But I'm tryin' to stay away from red meat and fries, the wife says it's got too much cholesterol. So I had the turkey club, more my speed."

"Food's consistently good."

"Yeah."

"Thought you'd enjoy a good smoke to celebrate the arrival of the little man."

"Well, you know I can't smoke at home now!"

And the two laughed heartily, flapping their wings and poking each other in the belly with their feet.

I stood transfixed, in utter awe. They were so agile, they could move so freely, and yet still had the ability to prevent the cigars from falling out of their beaks. It was as if they were dancing! What am I saying? They were dancing!

Like Fred and Ginger, cheek to cheek, one cigar headed one way and the other cigar headed the other way, they were dancing to a melody I could not hear. In perfect syncopation, they glided along the roof near the driver's side window, more like tightrope walkers than dancing birds, wings wrapped around each other, feathered bellies touching.

Suddenly, the dance became more frenzied, taking them into the air, still cheek to cheek, but wings flapping now, propelling them up, up, up…until all I could see were two red embers towering above East 74th

Street. I surmised the pigeons were headed toward some unknown luxury high-rise nest, where puffing away, they would joke into the first light, the sunrise illuminating the ripples of smoke from their cigars as it dispersed into the morning sky, the two continuing to sit, luminous, wrapped in ribbons of pink light, elevated far above the human scratching noises below.

Birds have always played an important role in my life. One evening, as I lay in my childhood bedroom, four birds flew in the window.

They had ribbons in their beaks which they wrapped around the bedposts. When the ribbons were securely fastened, they lifted the bed, with me in it, into the air, and we floated, quite effortlessly, out the window.

We flew by Marion's house, close enough that I could look through the window to see her asleep in her bed. Then we flew higher, above the clouds where the sky was blue and the sun was warm and shining.

When we started to descend, we flew through Aunt Peggy's windows and landed in her living room. I could hear the voices of Uncle Herman and my parents. Sylvia and her husband, George, were also present. They all sat in the dining room seemingly talking about adult things as they always had, the singsong quality of their voices accompanied by the clatter of forks and knives against plates. The air was filled with the aroma of roasted meat. I realized, quite slowly at first, that they were talking about me. They were criticizing me in great detail. Not a single one of them had a kind word to say.

I started to jump out of bed; I wanted to run into the dining room to defend myself, to tell them that they were wrong! But just as I stepped out of the bed, the birds lifted it off the ground and we were sky bound again.

Up above the clouds, the birds said that they had showed me something I had needed to see. That I was to do nothing until the time was right. I asked them when might that be, and how I would know. And they responded that I would know the time was right when I felt it in my bones. I suggested that might be when I was very old. And they said perhaps, or maybe sooner.

Suddenly, we were flying through the souk in Jerusalem! Obviously, the birds had been there before, because everyone knew them and greeted them warmly. We were offered dark, sweet tea with cardamom. I sat drinking the tea while the birds negotiated a trade: the bed for a flying carpet.

The birds insisted that for the next leg of the journey, because it was so very far and they would grow tired, a magic carpet would be a more comfortable means of transportation.

When the choice was finally made, I sat upon the most beautiful Oriental carpet I had ever seen, made of millions of delicate silk threads in earthy shades of red, green, brown, and gold. The carpet was luxurious, elegant, and smooth. The colors, although subdued earth tones, had a silky texture and a marvelous sheen.

The birds and I sat marveling at the carpet and discussing our good fortune while drinking our sweet, dark tea. The owners had served dates and dried figs alongside on a small silver plate. The meat in both was so sweet and rich it was difficult to imagine that once it had been fruit, growing on a tree.

Finally, the birds began circling overhead, signaling that it was time to go. We said good-bye to the store owners, who hugged us all and wished us well. As a going-away present, the shop owners prepared a small carpetbag filled with dates and figs for me, and another filled with nuts and seeds for the birds.

I sat on the carpet, the birds sitting on my shoulders and head, and slowly we began to rise. We rose high above the Old City of Jerusalem, flying over the Western Wall and the Dome of the Rock, up, up into the blue and above the clouds. The pungent smells and bright colors of the souk remained in my nostrils as I fell asleep.

When I awoke, we were in a vast plain filled with tall grass. The sky was purple, and off in the distance, as the sun began to sink into the earth, a pride of lions could be seen, the young ones romping and playing with the mother, who was lying down and appreciatively grooming her young when they came to sit by her side, while the father sat at the top of a hill, surveying his domain. All was peace.

The first stars began to flicker in the dark purple sky, and my senses were awake and alive with the aroma of earth, grass, and beasts. I made a fire of dried twigs and desert grasses and watched the moon rise over the plain. I was overcome by nature's majesty. After eating several dates, I fell asleep.

The magic carpet was entering my bedroom window, and ever so slowly the carpet transformed back into my bed. I sat upright, looking around the room. Everything was as it had been. The birds said their good-byes and promised to return very soon. I thanked them for my wonderful journey. Lying back on the down pillows, I fell fast asleep, hugging my carpet-bag full of dates.

When I awoke, I told my mother the story of my extraordinary night of flying around the world, and she insisted it was a dream. No matter how much or how hard I argued, she was adamant. I chose not to show her the bag of dates. That would remain my secret. Somehow, the birds must have known, because they never came to see me again, until now. I have taken that little bag everywhere I've ever been.

Diary Entry

NYC
December 24, 1973

"What's your earliest memory?" said the therapist.

The ghost considered her question for several minutes.

"Standing at the open door of our apartment with my mother and grandmother."

"How old are you?"

"Three."

"What are you doing?"

"Translating."

"Translating?"

"Yes, are you hard of hearing?"

"No. What is going on?"

"At the door?"

"Yes, at the door."

"Exactly?"

"Yes."

"A neighbor has come to the door asking to borrow a cup of milk."

"And?"

"And neither my mother nor my grandmother spoke English. So, they didn't understand what she wanted."

"And then what happens?"

"I translate her request into German. Then I translate their response into English. And on and on."

"Was this an unusual situation?"

"I was told that was the moment when my mother realized I spoke English. I had learned it from the neighbor's kids. From then on, I became the official translator."

The therapist was busily writing her notes, but beneath her calm exterior she was wondering what sort of woman doesn't know her child is fully bilingual for three years. Instead of offering this question to the patient, she cleared her throat.

"That's a lot of responsibility for a three-year-old."

"Came with the territory."

"Did you enjoy that position?"

"I guess it made me feel important. And needed."

"Did they eventually learn to speak English?"

"My grandmother never did. Although I think she understands everything that people say to her."

"How long has she been in the country?"

"Twenty-three years."

"What else do you remember?"

"My sister."

Now, the therapist looked up and stopped writing notes on her legal pad. She took off her glasses and focused her full attention on the ghost.

"Please tell me about her."

My ghostly self looked out the window.

"Lizzie is fantastic. She has long, wavy red hair and startling turquoise eyes. She is an artist, a painter. She's working on a red series, an Ode to Rothko. She lives on the West Coast."

"Did she come to the funeral?"

"No."

"Why not?"

"She and my mother never got along."

"Still, you would think she'd have paid her last respects."

Silence.

"Do you have a photo of her?"

"They're in storage."

"You don't keep a photo of her?"

"She's in my mind. That's where I keep her." The ghost continued gazing out the window. Then she said, "It's snowing."

"How do you feel about that?"

"It's peaceful. It makes the city quiet and white."

"You seem tense."

"I don't want to talk anymore today. I want to walk in the snow."

Illusion of Memory

Chapter 22

Diary Entry

Jerusalem
January 1, 1974

An Arab man walks down a side street in the Old City of Jerusalem. Although the street is paved, the houses are constructed of very old stone. Behind him can be seen an archway, like the entrance to a small tunnel, beyond which lies the souk, which at midday is filled with merchants and tourists.

The Arab man wears a light-colored beret, a ragged dark suit, and a pale collarless shirt buttoned to the neck. He sports a carefully groomed mustache and under his arm carries a package wrapped in brown paper and carefully tied with string.

Illuminated by the light coming through the archway, he makes his way slowly down the street. There is an apartment built into the top of the archway, two stories above the street, which has three small, thick, leaded windows, one of which is open. Iron bars are cemented into the top and bottom of the windows. In the room beyond, the imprisoned can be heard singing. Sheer silk curtains of pale pink move in the hot breeze which carries on it the soft sound of women's laughter.

To the right of the man carrying the paper bag stand two men in their early twenties. The one on the right holds a cigarette in his left hand, which he flicks nervously while he chats abstractedly with another man, who counts worry beads in his right hand. The two men, who stand no more than six inches apart, look at each other uncomfortably.

Several storefronts close for lunch. The light reflects off stained-glass windows, cutting across the street, like illustrated rays of God. The man carrying the package leaves the Old City by the northern gate, and walks to the center of the New Jerusalem. He smokes one unfiltered French cigarette after another, until he arrives at the bus station, where he purchases a one-way ticket to Beersheba and heads to the men's room.

Carefully placing the package on the floor, he relieves himself. Then, taking the package with him and placing it on the windowsill above the sink, he washes his hands and dries them on a dirty, overused, damp towel. He looks around the room and chooses a spot above the last lavatory, directly above the toilet. After placing the package there, and prior to leaving, he examines himself in the mirror one last time. Pleased with what he sees, he walks out into the bright sunlight, and walks through the proper gate where he boards the bus headed south.

Twenty minutes later the Arab man looks at his watch, then gazes lovingly at the hills outside Jerusalem. He says a prayer to Allah and, playing with his worry beads, he bows his head to his chest and sighs.

Outside the bus station, there are fifty dead and seventy-five injured from the blast that originated in the men's room. The walls left standing are covered in blood, and the cries of women and children can be heard above the din of the police cars and ambulances racing to save those left behind.

Moments earlier, Gidon, having survived his Egyptian captors, stood by as his fiancée boarded a sherut taxi headed for Haifa, where she was visiting her little brother who studied architecture at the Technion.

Gidon waved until the taxi was out of sight before turning away and walking toward his car. He considered himself a lucky man. He was marrying a wonderful woman who loved him, there were plenty of other girls who adored him, and today was his first day back at his art gallery.

He was lucky to have had a sister who minded the store for him while he was held prisoner by the Egyptians. He was incredibly glad to be back in the flow of real life.

There was joy in his step as he fumbled in his pockets for the car keys. Despite the continued bruising ache in his back and sides where the Egyptians had beat his kidneys, he felt good. Catching a glimpse of his reflection in the café windows, he thought perhaps he should have a quick coffee. Never know whom you might meet.

As he took a step toward the café door, the blast from the men's room blew the glass out of the windows, sending shards flying into the crowd. A sharp triangular piece of glass careened sideways into the air like a phantom jet, severing Gidon's head at the base of his neck. Within seconds, his body lay buried beneath piles of stone and glass from the collapsed building, while his head sat atop a pile of rubble ten feet away, his eyes staring out into space.

Diary Entry

NYC
January 11, 1974

The ghost sits in the therapist's office in silence. If she had a machine gun, she would be a statistic. Violent fantasies dominate her waking hours. She debates whether or not to confess her rage, her pain, her disappointment, but she cannot speak.

The letter explaining Gidon's death lies in her lap. Her hands rest limply on either side. She has retreated. Life and her sense of loss and outrage are too painful to bear.

The therapist enters, wiping her mouth with the back of her hand, the smell of just eaten food clinging to fine silk clothes. She looks at her patient who is staring out the window with glazed eyes.

"How are you?" she asks.

Silence.

"Has something happened?"

Silence.

The ghost hands the letter to the therapist and continues gazing out the window. The therapist reads.

Silence.

She looks up at her patient.

"I'm terribly sorry."

Silence.

The ghost wonders how sorry terribly might be, but says nothing.

It is raining. Outside, buses are honking loudly, cab drivers are swearing, and the city glistens as the first lights of evening illuminate the sky. *It would be fine, she muses, if I never spoke again. What is there to say, and who would listen?*

"I care about you, Betty."

Yeah, as long as you get that check every week.

"Please, let me in?"

Must I?

"Would you like to stay here tonight?"

Yuck.

"I have a guest bedroom. No one would disturb you. And I'd be down the hall if you needed me."

Gazing, gazing, gazing. The rain in Spain. Tomorrow and tomorrow and tomorrow creeps…oh, Billy boy.

"You're drenched. Why don't you take a hot bath and let me give you some dry clothes? You look terrible."

Mary, Mary, quite contrary, how does your garden grow?

"Betty, can you hear me?"

Tommy, can you hear me? Tommy, can you see me? Too bad I'm not a pinball wizard, I could be rich and famous and the lot of them could go to hell.

"Betty?"

Betty? When the hell did I become Betty? The name is Bette.

"I need for you to speak."

Or what?

"Or I'll be forced to call the hospital and have you admitted, and I don't want to do that."

That's a thought. Three meals a day. Drugs forever. Plenty of sex. My father would be so happy. Sylvia would marry him and...

"Fucking hell."

"What did you say? I couldn't hear you."

"I'll be damned if I let you or them put me away for the rest of my life. Fucking hell."

"You need to take a bath."

"Why?"

"You smell."

"So?"

"And you're filthy."

"Yeah?"

"When did you eat last?"

"I don't remember."

"I'll have Ella run you a bath."

"Ella Fitzgerald is running my bath? Would she sing for me?"

"It's Ella, my maid."

"Does she sing the blues?"

"I've never asked her."

"You should."

"I'll bear that in mind. Do you prefer lavender or orange blossom?"

"Tea?"

"Bath salts."

"Lavender."

"Follow me."

"Why?"

"I'm going to show you to your room."

"I didn't agree to stay."

"You'll need a place to change out of your wet clothes in order to take a bath, and a place to dress again after, won't you?"

"I suppose I will."

"Good, then. It's settled."

"No funny stuff."

"What do you mean, 'funny stuff'?"

"Like wanting to scrub my back or anything like that."

"No. No funny stuff."

"Promise me?"

"I promise."

"Does the bathroom door have a lock?"

"It does."

"And a telephone?"

"Yes."

"How about a TV?"

"No TV permitted in the bath, sorry."

"How about a waterproof radio?"

"Both FM and AM."

"OK."

"OK, what?"

"I'll take a bath if I can lock the door and play loud classical music on the FM station, and if no one disturbs me."

"Is that what you want?"

"Yes."

"Deal?"

"Deal."

Illusion of Memory

Roberta's Journal Entry

NYC
January 11, 1974

When Elizabeth arrived for her session today, she scared me out of my wits. She looked as if she's been living on the street. And it was clear to me from her behavior that she was having a nervous breakdown.

I could barely look at her; she looked and smelled so awful. But I also couldn't bear to send her back out into the world. It's been raining and very cold. She arrived without a coat, wearing a sweater and jeans, soaked to the skin, and absolutely filthy. I responded in a way that goes against my training.

I suggested she take a hot bath and allow Ella to launder her clothes.

Then I recommended she stay in the guest room overnight. I feel absolutely correct in my judgment. Now, I am waiting for Dr. Blau to return my call so that we can discuss what has happened.

I knew that in that moment, I could have proceeded in a detached therapeutic way, or with great compassion as my soul was screaming for me to do. To proceed in a detached and therapeutic way lacked spirit. It was robbing us of the opportunity to be truly human. So I reached out.

Elizabeth has lost another friend in a bombing accident. Her aunt and father want her out of the way so they can officially claim her inheritance, or what will be left of it when they're done running through it.

There is no question that she needs a therapist. But more than a therapist, she needs a friend who won't abandon or betray her.

She is ill and so vulnerable. And if I am able to protect her, why should I deny her that protection? I can balance my more tender feelings toward her, knowing that under my roof, she is safe from harm. And I know that by staying here, she will definitely be safe and warm.

I was brought up a strict Catholic, but I believe in the here and now. I don't think Elizabeth should die on a park bench of pneumonia so that she can go to a better place. A Jewish friend once said that according to the Talmud, to save a life is the most important thing one can do in one's lifetime. That resonated for me the moment I heard it. But I did not understand it as fully then as I do now.

I grew up in a charitable and kind home surrounded by good people. I can only pray that, should my life change, should I suddenly find myself in Elizabeth's place, a kind soul would extend a helping hand to me.

Therefore, if I must choose between being a commendable therapist or a decent human being, I choose the latter. If the therapeutic community finds my behavior inappropriate, so be it. I would rather sell lox at Zabar's for the rest of my life than spend my days haunted by what I should have done. If I turned her away, I'd never be able to live with myself.

So there it is. My Catholic religious upbringing, everything I've rebelled against by becoming a therapist, has bitten me in the ass. As I looked at Elizabeth I had an odd thought. Something from the past came up, something I haven't thought about for years. When I was a child, my Polish mother would recount a particularly poignant story from the war.

A close friend and neighbor, a woman she had gone through school with, came to see my mother and begged for a place for her family to hide. She suggested the root cellar of the house. She was Jewish and wanted to hide from the Nazis. She was so desperate, and she offered to pay.

My mother was conflicted about what to do, and asked for twenty-four hours to think it over. The next morning, the woman and her family were arrested and taken to a concentration camp, where they all died.

As I looked at Elizabeth shaking in the chair of my therapy room, it struck me that my mother and I owed her this protection. We only get so many chances to get it right. And I found myself thinking that it was no mistake that she was my patient and that she was here right now. God had brought her to me, and this time, I could not and would not turn her away.

Chapter 23

Diary Entry

NYC
January 12, 1974

The bathroom had black and white tiles on the floor, a high ceiling, and a claw-foot tub filled almost to the brim with steaming water and lavender bath salts. There were so many small soaps; rose, lavender, patchouli, and sandalwood, each in its own dish. The tiles on the walls were white, with a line of black around the top, and there was a huge window that looked out across the park's bare treetops all the way to Fifth Avenue. The streets shimmered and a light mist formed halos around streetlamps. The window was open at the top, from which the breeze brought in the smell of the pavement and damp earth.

I stripped off my clothes and sank into the bath water. Lying on the bottom of the tub, I could see straight up to the ceiling while my hair fanned out around me. Sitting on the chair beside the tub were two big fluffy pale pink towels and a waterproof radio. Finding WQXR, I sank beneath the water again, to see how it would feel to listen to the music from under water.

With the flick of a switch, Bach Partitas were

bouncing off the walls and echoing in the high-ceilinged room. I was catapulted into another century, where I was a handmaiden to the queen. Then, under water once again, the music sounded softer, as if it were being played by an orchestra of mermaids in an underwater concert hall.

I was swimming with my father and laughing, and spraying my childhood friend Marion Cohn's face with water, while my mother reclined beside the pool looking like Ava Gardner, wearing dark glasses and sunbathing, her lips and toenails a glamorous red, her bent arm and delicate ringed fingers holding a smoldering cigarette.

There was a knock at the door that sounded like thunder. I dove deeper under the water.

"The doctor wants me to tell ya that dinner will be ready in half an hour, Miss Bette," said Ella from the other side of the door.

I turned down the radio. "Miss Ella?"

"Yes?"

"Do you sing?"

"In church."

"Would you sing for me?"

"I would, but I gots supper on the stove."

"Please? Sing for me now."

"I'd have to think about that, child."

"Please?"

Ella shuffled uncomfortably, not knowing what to

do.

"I s'pose a little gospel couldn't hurt."

"Yes!" I cried, clapping my hands.

"From right outside this door?"

"Yes, please."

Ella first cleared her throat, and then she started to hum the opening notes. "Hmmm, swing low, sweet chariot…"

Sinking down into the warm water, my body began to let go. Ella had a deep, throaty, rich voice that made the fear in my bones drain out through my toes. Her deep voice lulled me, the hot water calmed me. I drifted in and out. At the peaks, Ella's voice brought me back. To the lavender bath. To the steam. To the people who called themselves my family. I was their flesh and blood, their only child. I sank beneath the water and listened to Ella as if she were a siren luring me to her.

"I'll be goin' now," said Ella when she'd finished. "Dinner's got to be watched."

The ensuing silence made me shudder. Looking at the medicine cabinet, I wondered whether it held razor blades or sleeping pills. Razor blades scared me. The blood and the pain scared me. The bath water turning red scared me. The more I considered it, the more sleeping pills seemed to be my style. I liked the thought of drifting away painlessly into a deep forever sleep. Razors implied violence, while pills seemed kind and gentle, closer to a real, unplanned death.

A loud knock at the door shook me out of my reverie.

"I've left some clean, dry clothes for you on the bed. I hope they fit. I've placed your wet things in the clothes washer. They'll be dry by the time dinner is over. Dinner is in fifteen minutes… You OK in there?"

"Yes."

"It's Ella's fried chicken night. Rather a *spécialité de maison.*"

The ghost burst into tears. They streamed down her ashen face into the bath water.

"You'll feel better after you eat. Do you need a hand?"

"No. Give me a few minutes."

"I'm down the hall if you need me."

The ghost heard the therapist walk away down the soft carpet of the hall. A violent internal fight erupted. The members of the committee were screaming at one another, "Be strong! Feel nothing! You pussy! You would never have survived Auschwitz! Pull yourself together!"

And like the ghost she was, she floated out of the bath and slowly started to dry her body. Catching a glimpse of someone in the mirror, she stopped to look. The woman in the mirror was bony and pale, with long blonde hair and large, sad blue eyes. Her eyes said that her world had been ripped away, that she had been abandoned, that she was destitute.

At the center of her chest was a gaping hole where her heart had been. The hole was so large that you could see the tiled wall behind her. And she knew at once that for the remainder of her life, people would feel they had the right to push her around. People would see the hole and would know that she was an easy mark; they could steal what they wanted, because there was no one who cared enough to protect and defend her. And because she had little recourse, strangers would take great pleasure in hurting her. Laughing, they would say, "You don't count. No one loves you enough to back you up. You are totally powerless and meaningless. And now, you're poor to boot!"

And as the ghost watched the image in the mirror dry herself, she thought, *That one? I would be surprised if she lasted the night.*

Diary Entry

New York City
January 13, 1974

The ghost sat on the toilet seat drying herself for a long time. She was filled with fear. But more than anything, she was exhausted from wondering what to do next. So she put her pink plush bath towel over the fluffy white bath mat next to the tub, lay down, curled up in the fetal position, and fell asleep while listening to the sound of the water going down the drain.

She dreamt she was high above the earth, circling the world on her magic carpet, accompanied by the pigeons she had seen smoking cigars and dancing on the hood of the BMW parked in front of her house.

"Nothin' like gettin' away," said one bird to the other.

"I know," the second said between puffs on his cigar. "Gives ya a whole new point of view."

"Like my shrink says, it kinda reframes your reality!" said the gray one, and let out a big belly laugh. The two pigeons sat beside each of Bette's ears as she lay on the magic carpet.

"You're missing the seven wonders of the world."

At which point Bette sat up, cross-legged.

"You're kind of a wonder of the world, if ya ask me!" said the scruffy pigeon.

"Sure," she said in her best world-weary tone.

"You don't get it, do ya?"

"What's there to get?"

"You've got something they can't take away."

"What's that?"

"Ya have to ask?" said one.

"You're an artist, aren't ya?" added the other.

"You can take whatever they do or say and transform it. And there's nothing they can do about it. And there's an endless supply they can never touch. Making art enriches you beyond your wildest dreams."

"I never thought of it that way," she replied.

"We know. That's why we took you on this little trip."

And the three laughed heartily, grabbing their bellies and laughing so hard that Bette awoke still laughing.

"Bette, are you OK in there?"

"Ha-ha-ha...yeah. Ha, yeah, I'll be right, ha-ha-ha, out."

And slowly, imperceptibly, Bette felt her soul reenter her body.

Chapter 24

Diary Entry

New York City
January 30, 1974

"Tell me about her."

"She is everything I am not," said Bette, squirming uncomfortably in her seat.

"How so?"

"She has tremendous daring. She is fearless. She takes risks."

"What are her relationships like?"

"She loves with abandon."

"Would you say she is excessive?"

"She has appetites."

"Does she fulfill those appetites?"

"Completely."

"Do you admire that quality in her?"

"Yes."

"Do you have appetites?"

"Yes."

"Do you act on them?"

"No."

"Why not?"

"I don't know."

"Your father says you never had a sister."

A deafening silence engulfs the room.

"He's lying," says Bette, and looks out the window. Across the street two Puerto Rican men are washing windows. She inhales and lets out a sigh.

"Did you make her up?"

Bette does not want to discuss this. No, definitely not. No entrance here.

"What difference does it make?"

"It's the difference between your freedom and being institutionalized for the rest of your life."

"This world and the people in it will never be what Lizzie and I need."

Roberta removes her glasses and places them on her desk. She is exasperated but determined. The ghost and the therapist sit facing each other in their separate chairs on opposite sides of the room, as if it were high noon at the OK Corral and this were the final shoot-out.

"It's OK to have created her, Bette," Roberta says.

"I don't need your approval."

"That's stone cold, but it isn't the truth."

"Absolutely the truth. I fly solo from here on in."

"You can't live without other people, Bette."

"I love humanity! It's only individuals I hate."

"You created her as a survival mechanism."

"Competent response, Doctor."

"Would you agree, she does all the things you wish you were strong enough to do? And she does not appear to need anyone else's acceptance? Is she always true to herself?"

Pause.

"Is she the unlived part of you?"

"Nope."

"Think about it."

"Je ne pense pas, donc je suis."

"I don't speak French. Please translate."

"I don't think, therefore I am."

"Clever."

"That's my middle name."

"I'd like to get back to the subject of your sister."

"She's a Zen riddle, you figure it out."

Illusion of Memory

Letter to Lizzie

NYC
February 3, 1974

Dearest Lizzie,

Well, it certainly has been the most difficult time. There I was, trying to help you remember our childhood, and look what has happened! I've remembered everything, and now you are off on a trip to Italy and keep missing my letters. Well, I hope you receive this one because I've had a revelation.

When I was in Jerusalem studying the Kabbalah, we read from the main Kabbalistic text, the Zohar, which happens to have been written in the 1300s. In it, four rabbis travel the world discussing the hidden meaning in the stories of the Talmud. If it weren't the truth, it would sound like a joke.

Well, in the text, the narrative of the beginning of the world is a bit different than the version of Genesis as we know it. The Zohar says that in the beginning, there was Ein Sof, literally "Without End," or infinity, into which the light of the world appeared, needing to give. In response, a vessel appeared needing to receive! However, the vessel soon discovered that it was not strong enough to contain all God's light, and it shattered.

The sexual imagery notwithstanding, the Kabbalistic conclusion is that no one and nothing can contain all God's light. We can only handle a little bit of light at a time, or we will shatter. Do you see? You and I have each had too much light! And the only way out is to climb the tree of life to the highest rung, or return to earth to live several more lifetimes—until we reach the highest level of our spiritual evolution, that is.

My soul has been flooded with light! I am a portal through which God's light pours, and alas, this vessel is too small. So I've shattered. My ego has exploded into a million glittering pieces. And yet, my therapist assures me that a new and more balanced version of myself is due to be born. Which is good news! Having been most recently with God, children are sacred beings. I wish to experience unprecedented intimacy with God.

You know, it never occurred to me that when the first rule of the Kabbalah was revealed—that nothing is as it seems—it was our lives the professor was talking about. The second rule, which is what is most hidden carries the greatest power, should have awakened me. But no, I slept on. Now I see that Mom chose a moment when I was closest to God. She was trying to steal my connection to God's light for herself!

And at that precise moment, the Angel of Darkness could have snatched both our souls, but he did not. Because God intervened and then made us forget.

While the act of remembering is a function of love, the act of telling is nothing short of flooding the family vessel with light. One can only speculate what form the shattering of our family vessel will take. By bringing this information to light, the family may insist that we are both crazy and only fit to be locked in the darkness for the rest of our days.

I just know that when I tell Dad what I remember, he will deny everything. I will ask, why didn't you protect me? He will shrug his shoulders and deny.

But oh, how sweet it would be to hear him say he was sorry.

I assume that the Dark Angel has inhabited our lives for quite some time. There is a silver lining, however: in the Kabbalah, evil is an aspect of the Divine! The Angel of Darkness must obtain permission from God to do his work. Of course, once permission is granted, he is free to destroy everything he sees.

Ironically, when a man and a woman marry, the female spirit of God establishes a presence in their home. This spirit is called the Schechinah.

When a man travels far from home, the Schechinah accompanies him for his protection. In our parents' marriage, in her stead, the Dark Angel took up residence.

Upon first seeing our parents' faces, he knew instantly that they belonged to him. When they traveled across the sea to America, he set up his headquarters in our home, feeling such comfort! After all, they insisted that God was dead, or perhaps had never existed, or had abandoned them when they needed him most. There existed the kind of congenially hopeless atmosphere the Angel of Darkness so adores. And so, the Dark Angel's warm presence accompanied us, sitting beside us where, by rights, the Schechinah should have been.

Perhaps the Holocaust was merely the twentieth-century equivalent of the flood? Maybe God looked down at his creations with such disgust that from one moment to the next, he knew unequivocally that water would not be enough. He had created something that had grown so evil, that he would create the needed darkness so that we would be forced to understand our need for transformation.

Apparently, when Noah spotted the Angel of Darkness among the people, he hid, thereby preventing the Angel from seeing his face. Our parents did the same. They hid behind false identities, making the first premise of the Kabbalah a reality; they were not what they seemed and were forced to pretend that they were not ashamed of what they had to become. At first, the Dark Angel passed them a thousand times a day. It was not until he sensed their shame that he took refuge in their souls. Once there, although he brought them comfort, they would never again be blessed in the spiritual world; like Esau, who had betrayed his brother, they could and would be blessed only in the material world.

If it is true that we are tested by God not because he needs another display of devotion, but by seeing the chink in the wall of our spirit, and having sent the Dark Angel on an excursion to tempt us, it is there that our opportunity for transformation resides. When God presents us with such an opportunity, it seems at first that it will be our demise. But no, in such moments we are asked to rise to the next level of our spirituality. If a solution can be found by considering everyone's greatest good, then that is considered a spiritually enlightened resolution, something which pleases God.

Whereas, a choice made for the betterment of one man's good alone is neither evolved nor acceptable. In choosing their particular path to save themselves, the pact was made.

Mom's death has created a space for the light to enter, which in turn has exposed Dad's long-standing affair, so to speak, with her sister, Sylvia. So you might ask, why has the truth chosen to appear at this particular moment? According to my therapist, it happens in families every seven generations. Even the statistics have mystical numerological connotations.

You and I have been cast out, and it is precisely through our exile that we are to be spared! Do you see? He has created our trial! If we are to heal ourselves, then we must participate in the Healing of the

Universe, or Tikkun Olam. That is God's plan for us. Because let's face it: left to our own devices, we would never have chosen this path.

I hope this letter finds you at your hotel in Florence, which has always been my favorite city in the world. And while you are there, don't forget to eat some bistecca Fiorentina for me, and shop for lots of beautiful clothes!

Love,
Ta Bête, Bette

Chapter 25

Letter to Bette

Hotel Viva Italia
Florence, Italy
February 6, 1974

Dearest La Bette,

What can I say? Florence is magnificent this time of year! The shops have all the latest fashions—they're always two years ahead of us, you know—and the food and the wine and the men are delicious!

Well, little one, what would I do without you? The sons of bitches! You may be younger, but you certainly are clever! Keep me in the loop and we'll figure out what to do next!

I'm here with Count Igor, a new Russian flame who speaks seven languages fluently and is showing me the sights as I've never seen them before! I mean, Michelangelo's David at the Uffizi is divine! He is beyond speech. Really.

I can't believe what you're going through. Why don't you come here? I'd love to see you, and we'd have such fun. Give the invite some thought, eh?

Hugs and kisses,
Contessa Lizabetta

Diary Entry

New York City
February 7, 1974

The days are starting to run into one another. The time for my therapy session is nearing. I can hear my therapist, Roberta, paddling down the hall to her office. And I am filled with such gratitude. What would have happened to me if she hadn't taken me in? I can't imagine.

Ella has placed my clean clothes from her recent laundry run in a pile on the dresser. Reaching for the clean clothes, still warm from the drier and smelling sweetly of detergent, gives me a sense of well-being. I pull on my jeans, a clean T-shirt, and some warm socks, and head for the therapy room.

When I enter, Roberta is sitting in her chair, writing notes on a legal pad. Her reddish wavy hair frames her face, and for the first time since I've known her, she looks pretty in a bookish sort of way. She is wearing the beige outfit from our initial meeting, but has removed her shoes and is unconsciously rubbing her stocking feet against the carpet. I quietly take my seat, which creaks a bit when I sit down. She continues to scribble.

"Your father called. He has asked me to tell you that he would like to invite you to Montauk for the weekend." She looks up.

"Our summer house in Montauk? It's February," I say.

"I think it may be an opportunity."

"Really?"

"To connect."

"And say what? 'Oh, and by the way, Dad, I've remembered the first twelve years of my life'?"

"That might not be the best place to start."

"He does not want to know what I remember."

"If you choose not to tell him, the opportunity will be lost. You're already in exile, what more can he do?"

"I've been thinking a great deal about what I studied in Jerusalem in my Kabbalah class. It stressed that we need the right person to interpret our dreams. That person should either love or care about us. Or be a person who cares profoundly for all humankind."

"Is that your way of telling me you've had a dream?"

"Yes."

"I appreciate your confidence in me."

"Who said anything about confidence? I have a recurring dream, as opposed to an incorrigible dream that I have had since Lizzie lost her memory."

"Lizzie does not exist."

"How would you know? Did you know that simply by looking at something, it changes? That's a law of physics. And the more people look at an object, the more versions of reality come into existence. So who is to say that your version of reality is correct?"

"Your father wants to put you away for your version of reality."

"Does that make my reality any less real?"

"No."

"Precisely."

"However, in the relative world, you must admit that being free is better than being institutionalized."

"I'm not so sure."

"Please trust me on that."

"In order to save myself I must say that Lizzie does not exist, is that correct?"

"Correct."

"Doesn't that pretty much put us back in the Dark Ages, when Jews had to give up their belief in the one Hebrew God or be killed? What if I am a mystic and Lizzie is the Schechinah?"

Roberta looks over the tops of her glasses and smiles. "Then, I'm the Queen of the Nile."

"Your Majesty."

"Unfortunately, this is not a joke."

"Sure."

"All right, play your little game. Only remember: unless you are willing to say that Lizzie does not exist, your father and aunt will have you locked up where even I and Dr. Blau can't get access to you."

Bette considered the news for a moment.

"Who contacted you?"

"Their attorney."

"And?"

"They want you to sign an agreement saying you're crazy, and they want me to sign one saying you are delusional."

"That's ridiculous! I'd have to be crazy to sign it."

"If you want me not to sign, you had better fess up that Lizzie does not exist."

"And my inheritance?"

"My sense is they are spending it so fast, it would be a miracle if there were anything left by the end of the year."

"Must I go to Montauk?"

"Think about it and let me know by tomorrow afternoon."

"Mind if I ask you how much you get paid per visit?"

"What difference does it make?"

"I would like to know, please."

"One hundred seventy-five dollars per hour."

"Twice weekly. Four weeks a month. That's my money they're spending, you know."

I've been thinking about that. How would it be if I used it to help you get your own place?"

"I think I'm delusional. I could swear I just heard you say you'd like to help me get my own place."

"I did."

"Why?"

"Just start looking, OK?"

"That's not good enough."

"Someone has to help you get a start. It might as well be me."

"Touching."

"You have every right to feel skeptical."

"I don't know what to say."

"That must be a first."

I look away, embarrassed by my vulnerability.

"Let's talk about the dream."

"Why do I feel embarrassed by your kindness?"

"You're not used to it. It takes time."

"I feel undeserving."

"That's understandable. Let's focus on the dream, shall we?"

"I dreamt that my mother came to my bed."

The therapist nods and starts to write.

"I only see her from the back. She is wearing a long, pale, satin nightgown to the floor, it looks like something Jean Harlow would have worn in one of her 1940s movies, with a low back, and her clean dark brown hair is brushing her shoulders. I see her manicured hand lift up the covers as she slides into bed next to me. I feel her body against mine, her nipples are rubbing against my arm, and it feels as if she is pregnant, her belly is big and round and hard against my back. Her hands search out my thighs, roll me over and spread them apart. She starts furiously rubbing my clitoris. It is very exciting. When I turn to look at her face, I see a death mask. It is her face frozen at the moment of her death. I am repulsed, and jump out of bed. Then I wake up. Usually panting and sweating."

"How many times have you had this dream?"

"About ten since I've been here."

"How does it make you feel?"

"Disgusting. When I wake, I feel sexually aroused, but when I realize what I've been dreaming, I feel revulsion and shame. And the more often I dream the dream, the more disgusted I feel."

"Was your mother ever pregnant after you were born?"

The room started to feel as if the walls were closing in on us.

"I don't remember."

"Is there anyone you could ask?"

"I don't know."

"Think about it."

I don't want to think about it. I change the subject.

"You know, my ex-husband, Peter, was just like her."

"In what way?"

"He pretended to be someone he was not. He was handsome and well dressed, and like her, he flirted with anyone and everyone regardless of sex. He also pretended to be affluent when he was poor."

"And he used you as a beard, just the way your mother did on that trip to Europe."

"I never thought of that."

"I'm so sorry this has happened to you."
"Don't do that! Don't pity me!"
"It could have been worse."
"How?"
"I don't know, but it can always be worse."

Chapter 26

Letter from Aunt Peggy

New York City
February 7, 1974

Dearest Bettylein,

Dear old Tante Peggy was thinking of you. So I
called your papa he gave me your address.

You should know that the entire family is talking
about Sylvia. She went to Israel. While she was there,
she visited all the extended family members and promised that she would leave them something (that should
have been yours) in her will. She thinks she's still nine-
teen, and she ran around telling anyone who would listen that every cab driver was flirting with her and
wanted her, and she told horrible lies about you. She
said she read your diary and that you are crazy, that
you sleep with women, and much, much more terrible
things. She was always crazy but now she is even
worse. The things she says are dirty and disgusting.

I am writing to you because I must tell you something about your mother's family: the Fuhrmann family. Your great-grandmother Fuhrmann, your
grandmother Berta's mother, she and her sisters and

her brother, David, ran the most successful bordello in all Czernovitz. I telling you this because the kind of behavior that Sylvia shows is not unusual for a woman who comes from such circumstances. I do not excuse what she do, but you have brains and maybe you can understand her?

Your father, on the other hand, has no excuse. Only that he is an idiot. First he fall in love with your mother because she was very beautiful, and later with Sylvia. But on the inside, they are all very ugly.

That is why my Herman, your mother's uncle, never embrace neither your mother nor Sylvia. Herman, your grandfather Joseph Honigsberg's brother, met your grandmother Berta when he had his own orchestra and she was working in the bordello. She became pregnant, so one night her brother David waited for your grandfather with a rabbi, and boom, they was married.

Your grandfather's parents, Herman's parents, met their pregnant daughter-in-law when they was making a *spaziergang* through the park.

Can you imagine? Hallo, Mama and Papa Honigsberg, meet my pregnant wife, Berta! Ha! It was a story for the books.

You can imagine, in those days, a Jewish woman to be pregnant before marriage was a great shame for the family. For Berta it was fantastish. She married a handsome and successful man, seven years younger, a talented, classical musician who came from a very prominent, successful, and established German Jewish family.

My side, the Honigsbergs, were the complete opposite of your mother's family. The Fuhrmanns were always fighting; over men, over money, over everything. There was never a moment of peace, always intrigues. And Sylvia is like her mother, Berta, *sie ist eine intrigantine*. She is making much intrigues and trouble for everybody.

I say these things because I know you must feel very bad. Do not give up hope! You are young and beautiful and talented, and you will make a life even with all the terrible things that Sylvia and your father has done. You will see that I know what I am talking about.

You are around the corner, so please call old Aunt Peggy on Riverside Drive, and come over and I will show you my photo albums of when I was young and beautiful. I had a very interesting life. I was a chanteuse, you know, and you will be surprised how many stories I will tell you. I hope you remember how fantastic a cook I am, so when you come I will make for you my famous stroganoff!

I kiss and hug you,
Your old Tante Peggy

February 9, 1974

BY HAND

Peggy Honigsberg
79 Riverside Drive
New York, NY

Dearest Aunt Peggy,

I was so happy to hear from you and would like so much to accept your offer to sample your famous beef stroganoff! Would you also make pelmeni and soup?

I very much look forward to seeing the photos of your career!

I will call you in the morning and we will make arrangements.

Many hugs,
Bettylein

Diary Entry

NYC
February 10, 1974

    I lie in bed in the pale early morning light listening to the garbage trucks go from house to house, picking up the trash along Central Park West. I reread Aunt Peggy's note. In the back of my mind I'm thinking, we produce so much garbage, certainly there must be a scientist somewhere who can convert it into something positive we can use? Of all the family, she has been the only member to contact me. I can't help wondering whether someone put her up to it, or whether she did it on her own.

    My mind travels across town and I imagine my father and Sylvia fast asleep in the brick building in which I grew up. My mother's piano silent; closed. Once again, I wish that God had taken me in the night.

    The committee is awake and in full swing.

    "You pussy," hisses a woman's voice, "you never would have survived Auschwitz. Go on," she croaks, "cry like a baby. *Yeke potz.*"

    Wily Polish and Romanian Jews would make fun of the Germans. Their directness and honesty were an affront, so they affectionately dubbed them, Yeke, meaning German in Yiddish, and potz, meaning putz. The demeaning term implied that you were not only naive, but stupid, because in their version of reality no one gets what he/she needs or wants by simply asking for it. You have to manipulate circumstances and people into giving you what you want. If you are really good, you can even make them think it was their idea!

"You idiot! You have to manipulate people!"

I think of the words of Theodore Herzel, but this morning his words give little comfort. Bearing that in mind, when my mother, who was Romanian, wanted me to shut a window, she would say, "Oh, it's so cold in here!" And then she would rub her arms with her hands, and just for good measure she'd shiver a bit. If I did not respond, she would follow-up with, "Bette, aren't you cold?"

That was my cue.

"Mom, would you like me to shut the window?"

To which she would reply, "What a good idea!"

If she was lonely or bored, her favorite trick was to wait until I'd gone to bed. Then she would wake me with a hysterical cry, "Bette! Come here, I need you!"

Believing something awful had happened, I would jump out of bed in a panic and run down the hall to her bedroom, to find her sitting up in bed wearing her finest satin bed jacket, face gleaming with night cream, arms crossed over her breasts, her eyes glued to the television.

My heart racing, I'd say, "What is it?"

And she would look up at me calmly and say,
"Would you shut off the TV?"

"You woke me up and got me out of bed to shut off your TV?"

"Yes."

"Shut off your own damn TV!"

"But Bette, you're already here!"

I'd storm off in a huff, and she would laugh. Then using the remote, she'd turn off the television.

"What do you want out of life?" she'd ask.

"A beach house in California," I'd say, "and a red convertible."

"That's all?"

"That's all."

"You're a *gutte neshumeh*. A good soul. What do you want to do with your life?"

"I want to paint and write."

"That's all?"

"Yes, Mom, that's all. And have lots of kids."

"Where did you come from?"

"What do you mean?"

"Nothing."

To honor my ancestors, I will perform my version of this Romanian manipulation. To gain my freedom, God will forgive me if I claim that Lizzie does not exist. When in truth, I know that she is my Schechinah, my protection, and God's presence.

Chapter 27

Diary Entry

NYC
February 11, 1974

I once saw a beautiful, unpretentious stone house on a tree-lined street in Q'var Schmeryahoo, a suburb of Tel Aviv that smelled of acacia and overlooked the Mediterranean. In that house with the marble floors, I imagined a happy life with a dark-haired husband, a good man who adored me and made me laugh, our three or four children, three or four cats and two dogs, enough land for several horses, and a study filled with books where I would write all day into the early afternoon. Although I had no idea where that image came from, I believed that if I held on to it, eventually the reality would imprint itself on the material world.

Now, when I sit at my desk listening to the hum of traffic and blare of horns in the street below, I wonder whether I would be able to return to that world, and if I did, knowing what I now know, whether I would consider myself worthy of it.

I ask my therapist, "How long will these feelings of worthlessness linger?"

"They might linger a long time, or be gone in a

week, it depends."

"On?"

"It varies from person to person."

I felt she was being kind. So I said something to get her attention.

"I thought a good place to start might be to haul my soul back from the edge of the abyss. The only problem is the abyss, like the universe, has no beginning and no end."

She did not rise to the bait.

"It really does vary."

Letter to Bette

Hotel Viva Italia
Florence, Italy
February 12, 1974

My dearest Bette,

You don't know me, but I am a friend of your sister's. I am very sorry to be writing this news to you, but this past Saturday afternoon, your sister leapt out her bedroom window to her death. She was visiting Florence with me and we were having the most romantic time, when she informed me that she could fly. Walking over to the window, she stepped up and flung herself out into the night air before I could stop her.

In her will, a glitter-encrusted note she carried everywhere with her, she requested that all her paintings and clothes be burned in a giant bonfire in the center of the town square, surrounded by her friends and colleagues from the hotel, and she wished to be cremated simultaneously. Well, needless to say, I had to fly everyone over and have the hotel in California crate her paintings and airlift them. The papers here covered the event as a funereal happening extraordinaire and it got a great deal of press. I've enclosed an article. I don't know whether or not you read Italian, but it is very complimentary and gave your sister the sendoff she deserved. I have enclosed a snapshot of the bon-fire; it is inside the urn.

You may have noticed that the urn is a bit light. Unfortunately, after the bonfire, while on my way to the post office to mail your sister's remains to you, an enormous gust of wind came up out of nowhere and blew the lid off. Her ashes literally went flying out the open taxi window. She never did like being confined.

Out the window twice strikes me as a message, don't you agree?

Lizzie once showed me photos of your artwork. I always thought the subject matter was a bit odd. But you have an extraordinary sense of color and composition.

My condolences to you on your loss. I will miss her tremendously. She was an entertaining and intelligent traveling companion, and a divine lover and friend. All our colleagues from the hotel will miss her jovial spirit and creative genius.

Yours truly,
Count Igor of Transylvania

Chapter 28

Diary Entry

NYC
February 12, 1974

In this morning's mail, I received a letter. It would seem I've won a Fulbright Scholarship. I want to go to Europe to paint. Perhaps I'll find a studio in Paris or Berlin. With everything that has happened, I had completely forgotten about the application. A trip seems destined. I will have to tell Roberta and show her the letter from Count Igor as proof of my transformation.

"I'm thinking of moving to Europe."

"Why Europe?"

"I applied for a grant a little over a year ago and totally forgot about it. An acceptance letter arrived today. I've received a Fulbright."

Roberta looked up and eyed me over the tops of her glasses. She was questioning what I had just told her and deciding how best to verify the information. I reached into my rear right jeans pocket and pulled out the letter.

"I thought I'd bring it along so you could see it," I said, and handed it to her.

She took a few minutes to read it, and then a smile

slowly crossed her lips as she started to laugh. "Oh my God! That's fantastic!"

"I'm talented!"

"Oh, Bette! This is wonderful!"

"Yes, it's good timing."

"We both have a lot to do."

"I have something else to show you."

I reached into the other back pocket and pulled out the letter from Count Igor. Once again, Roberta affixed her glasses to the perfect spot on her nose and read. She was smiling even more broadly. I could see all her front teeth.

"This letter says that Lizzie is dead." Roberta looked up at me in utter amazement.

"Yes."

"I guess I'll be drawing up the papers?"

"Yes."

"I'm glad to see that you have reached this decision."

"Yes. I'm sad, but I think it's for the best."

"You'll be free of them now."

"I want to see my father, Aunt Peggy, and my grandmother before I leave."

"Would you like me to arrange for you to see them here? You could, you know."

"No thank you. You've been so incredibly kind. I want to be the one to go to them."

Letter to Lizzie

NYC
February 13, 1974

Dearest Lizzie,

My sweet old pie, hang on to your hat, you are not going to believe what I am about to tell you. Last night, I had dinner with Aunt Peggy—Did I Tell You How Beautiful I Was?—of 79th Street and Riverside Drive fame.

She looks terrific for an old lass from Riga. Her hair and nails were done, her lipstick was bright red, and her auburn hair was up in the beehive hairdo she's worn since we were children. The apartment had been cleaned that day so everything was spotless, and there were fresh long-stemmed roses all over. Her *pelmeni*, of course, were perfect, as was the stroganoff she had lured me with in the first place.

After dinner she brought out the photo albums. They were only supposed to be of her during her swinging career years, but there were photos of Mom and Dad, too, from when they had just come to America.

Everyone looked very affluent and glamorous. And she and I got to talking about Mom and what a pity it was that she had died so young, and suddenly Peggy said something astonishing.

"Did you know that your mother became pregnant with another man's baby?"

"While she was married to my father?"

"Yes. She was having an affair with an old acquaintance from Czernovitz, a doctor, while your father was working very hard to support everybody: your grandma, your mother, Sylvia, and you."

"What happened?"

"She wanted to leave your father and marry the doctor. But the doctor didn't want her."

"How old was I?"

"About two, maybe three. It was soon after we arrived in America."

"Did she have the baby?"

"First there was a big fight when your father find out. And your mother run out of the house and come straight to Uncle Herman in tears. And he tell her she must to return to her family, that she cannot have the other man's child."

"What did she do?"

"Sylvia arrange an abortion in New Jersey."

"An abortion?"

"*Ach*, it was terrible. But what did she think?"

"Please, Aunt Peggy, if there is more, tell me."

"She do this a few more times, with different men. Men that she and Sylvia share." Peggy let out a belly laugh. "Also, *das war ein schmutziges business! (So, that was a dirty business!)* Come, let's have ice cream."

And that was that. I ate the chocolate side and Peggy ate the vanilla portion of Breyers, and she told me stories about traveling with the orchestra and touring Siberia! Ha! Can you imagine doing a tour of Siberia? She entertained the troops, and when it snowed very hard, the wheels of the train would freeze, and she and Herman would lock themselves in their compartment with a bottle of vodka and have sex for days!

I guess you inherited more than a few qualities from her!

I'm starting to think about Europe. I hope my letter reaches you. I know you're traveling all over the place, so please write soon!

> Soon, XOXOXOXOXOXOXO
> Ta Bête,
> Bette

Chapter 29

Diary Entry

NYC
February 14, 1974
Valentine's Day

It was one of those freaky seventy-degree days that come along each February, when suddenly everyone in the park is wearing shorts and throwing Frisbees, and colorful kites filled the sky, and people came out of the woodwork. Hundreds of people strolling down the streets of Manhattan materialized as if out of nowhere.

Dad was sitting on a park bench in the sun, wearing what had come to be his uniform over the years: blue jeans, brown suede Gucci loafers, a freshly ironed, pale blue island cotton shirt, and over that, a navy cashmere V-neck sweater, and sunglasses. When I walked up to him, he had removed his old Vacheron Constantine and was winding it.

"Hi, Dad."

"Ah, you're here! Just a minute. I'm winding my watch."

After he had fastened the strap to his wrist again, he stood up and kissed me on the cheek. For the first time, it seemed that either I had grown or he had shrunk; I was a head taller.

"You look terrific!" he said, barely looking me over.

"So do you."

"When I look in the mirror I don't recognize that old man staring back at me!"

He shook his head and laughed.

"Surprisingly beautiful day," I said.

"Yes, feels like summer." The formality in his voice had an edge.

"I got great news today. I'm the recipient of a Fulbright grant. I'm leaving for Europe in a couple of weeks."

"Someone gave you a grant? To do what?"

"To paint."

"What do you know?"

We were walking slowly. The park was crowded.

"You seem surprised."

"I didn't think you were that talented."

I pretended not to hear his remark.

"How have you been?" I asked.

"How can I be?"

"I don't know. That's why I'm asking you."

"I miss your mother," he said, and looked down at the ground as if she were buried there.

I felt he was waiting for me to say the same. Instead, I said,

"I've been in therapy, you know."

"I know. I've been paying for it."

"With my money." I could feel the blood rush to my face.

"I didn't come here to fight."

"Have you spent it all?"

My question was met with silence.

"How do you like living on the West Side?" he asked.

"They have terrific foreign movie theatres and great Chinese food."

"I prefer American movies. Westerns. That's why I live on the East Side."

I stopped walking and turned toward him.

"At Mom's funeral, Grandma told me that you and Sylvia have been lovers for many years. Is that true?"

"Grandma told you that?" He let out a laugh.

"Yes."

"Can you imagine that?" He continued laughing.

"I can."

"Ha!"

"Well, were you?"

"That's incredible!"

"Dad!"

"Unbelievable!"

"I've remembered the first twelve years of my life."

He stopped and eyed me distrustfully.

"I didn't realize you couldn't remember."

"Well, I couldn't."

"So?"

"I've remembered some things I'd like to share with you."

Suddenly he pouted, looking like a little boy who was about to be punished.

"Let's sit down," I said, and pointed toward an empty bench.

Several moments went by in silence. He had stretched his legs out in front of him and crossed them at the ankles. His hands were behind his head. I didn't know how to begin. He put his head back and closed his eyes as if he were sunning himself.

"I remember Mom being pregnant. She had an affair with a man who used to come to the house and take us to Jones Beach, didn't she? She became pregnant with his child and had an abortion. Am I right?"

He suddenly pulled his legs in and sat up.

"Who have you been talking to?"

"My therapist."

"How could you remember something like that? What were you, two, three years old?"

"Three."

"I don't believe you. You talked to someone. Somebody told you!"

"There's more, Dad."

"I don't want to hear it!" He turned his back to me and crossed his legs, hanging off the side of the bench.

"At around the same time, she sexually abused me."

From his position at the end of the bench, he said, "That doesn't surprise me."

"It doesn't?"

"Not at all." Slowly, he turned around to finally look at me. "She had many affairs. She was the most interesting woman I ever knew."

I almost jumped out of my seat.

"You think sexually abusing children is interesting?"

He looked at me sheepishly and crossed his arms resting on his chest.

"No."

I could barely see his eyes through the dark glasses. But he was sitting rigidly, his knees apart and his heels flat on the ground.

"Do you realize that people who have been sexually abused in childhood remain emotionally crippled? Can you understand that?"

"What does this have to do with me?"

"Why did you leave me alone with her?"

"After all these years, you are blaming me?"

Wasn't that the line the Nazis used?

"I'm not blaming you. I'm holding you accountable. You knew what she was capable of."

He bent forward on his elbows and looked down at his shoes. There followed a terrible silence. I waited for his response. Birds chirped. Children laughed. Dogs barked.

He finally cleared his throat.

"The three women were too strong for me."

His chin fell to his chest, making him look even smaller. He had thick hair; it was wavy at the forehead like mine. He wore it parted on the side, and it was still dark, with only a bit of gray at the temples.

"Why didn't you protect me?"

"They were too strong."

"You saved children during the war. You saved them from the Nazis. The children of strangers. Why did you protect them and not me?"

Still looking down, he shook his head as if to say no. Then he stood up, and pushing his hands deep into his jeans pockets, he slowly began walking as though he was just taking a break to look at an interesting plant and would return to finish our conversation. I remained seated, jostled by passersby, watching my father's small body recede into the crowd.

Chapter 30

Diary Entry

NYC
February 15, 1974

"How did it go?"
"I don't think he will ever speak to me again."
"What makes you say that?"
"He used a Nazi line on me."
"Which one?"
"After all these years, you blame me?"
"How did it make you feel?"
"Like shit."
"Why?"
"He was angry."
"You were very brave."
"I feel sick."
"Why?"
"He wasn't the least bit surprised that she'd abused me."

Roberta took a second to digest what I'd said.
"Maybe, you weren't the first."
"What?"
"If he wasn't surprised, it must have happened before."

"That's gross."

"The fact that he looked the other way makes him an accomplice."

I sat in Roberta's office watching the sun dance across her wall of books. She sat looking at me, occasionally stopping to write something in her notebook.

"What are you writing?"

She looked up.

"This has been a terrible thing for you to have to learn. You know, during the war, not having morals or ethics may have stood them in good stead. But postwar is another story. The irony is, of course, that your father saved the lives of other children, while neglecting his own. Unconsciously, your mother might have been jealous of the children he saved, and perhaps her abusing you was her way of leveling the playing field. That's speculation, but now that you have this perspective of them, how important is having their love and approval?"

"Not important."

Roberta, who usually kept her distance during our sessions, got up and pulled up a desk chair and sat beside me.

"You need to accept that you will never get what you need from them. It is like a death, and if you mourn it, I promise you will start to live your life without jumping through hoops. The only person's approval that really matters is yours."

"He's going to make me pay for this."

"He's been making you pay all your life."

"They are inside me."

"Yes."

"I want to get rid of them."

"I don't know whether that is possible. But you can pay attention to their voices, when they come up in your consciousness, when they speak to you as members of the committee. And you can talk to them and tell them to shut up."

"There's no going back, is there?"

"Would you want to?"

"Not really."

"This is your life's work."

Looking at Roberta, I sensed that she wanted to hold me in her arms, stroke my hair and tell me that everything would be all right. She wanted to be the mother I'd never had. I must have looked so fragile and forlorn. She gripped the arms of the chair with both hands. We looked at each other, knowing it would be a mistake if she reached out to me that way.

"What do you think I should do next?"

"I think you should put your life in order and get ready for Europe." Roberta stood up and walked back to her desk chair.

"I'm broke."

"You're not. The Fulbright is a hundred-thousand-dollar grant!"

"I mean, until I cash it."

"Besides, I'd like to buy a painting."

"One of my paintings?"

"Yes, the one you showed me of the three trans-vestites in full drag. How much would you like for it?"

I couldn't believe what Roberta was doing. I thought for a second and then blurted out my answer.

"Five hundred dollars."

"My dear, you've just sold your first painting!"

Letter to Bette

NYC
February 16, 1974

My dearest Bettylein,

I hope that you are well and happy?

I thought you would want to know that I sold the apartment in Manhattan, and have bought a beautiful, very large one-bedroom apartment in Forest Hills, Queens, near my cousin Adam. He and Marian are, after all, my only surviving family from Kutno, except for Helga, who lives in Switzerland. I have always considered Adam an older brother. And this way, Sylvia will only be a short twenty-minute subway ride away.

I sold Mom's piano. I assumed you would not want it since you are going to Europe, and it made me too sad to have to look at it every day.

I am planning to visit an old childhood friend. He moved to Australia after the war and lives in Melbourne with his wife and two children. Then, I will fly back via Switzerland to see Helga. She would like me to take an apartment in Thun and spend six months of the year near her. I am considering it.

Grandma is very sick. Sylvia has put her in a home on East 72nd Street and we have put her apartment on the market. Sylvia has decided to leave everything to her girlfriends, Lee and Alexandra, including the land in Montauk. There is no will, so she may be bluffing, but who knows? Litta's daughter Zeta made a special twenty-four-hour stopover on her way back to Israel from Europe. She has taken Mom's jewelry with her.

What shall I do with your paintings?

Much success in your endeavors, and please stay in touch.

Love,
Your Dad

February 17, 1974

Western Union Telegram

TO: LA LIZZIE c/o COUNT IGOR OF TRANSYLVANIA
HOTEL VIVA ITALIA
FLORENCE, ITALY

I KNOW YOU ARE ALIVE
STOP
I'M COMING TO ITALY
STOP
BE IN ROME IN LESS THAN 2 WEEKS
STOP
SOLD MY FIRST PAINTING
STOP
GRANDMA IS DYING
STOP
BITCH SYLVIA PUT HER IN A HOME
STOP
I LOVE YOU
STOP
YOURBABYSISTERTHEADVENTURESSBETTE

Chapter 31

Diary Entry

NYC
February 18, 1974

I received a phone call at the therapist's home at 4:00 a.m.

"Is this Bette Davis?"

"Yes."

"This is the Barnaby Home for the Aged. We're calling because your grandmother has had an accident. While the nurse was washing her, she fell out of bed and landed on her head. We cannot find your aunt Sylvia, so we are contacting you. We need you to come right away."

"Is she OK?"

"She's suffered a slight concussion. And has some cuts. We're very sorry."

"I'll be over right away."

The therapist was just as horrified as I at the news. I dressed hurriedly and headed for the door, zipping up my ski jacket. As she held the door open for me to leave, she pressed thirty dollars into my palm and insisted I take a taxi.

When I entered the room, Grandma was lying in

bed with an enormous bandage wrapped around her head.

"Oma? How do you feel?"

"Stupid idiot dropped me on my head."

"Do you have a headache?"

"She's a total pain in the ass."

"You don't like your nurse?"

"No."

"Do you want me to get you someone else?"

"Yes."

I took off my coat and sat in the chair next to her.

"What is the matter with you? Why are you here?"

"Because the beast Sylvia wants me out of the way. Take me home with you? Please? Get me out of here!"

I wanted to scoop her up in my arms and say, "Yes, Grandma, I'll take care of you."
But it would not have been true

"I'm living with friends. I got a grant and I'm going to Rome. I'm leaving in a few days."

"Since your mother died, there is no one to take care of me."

"What illness do you have?"

"Don't you see how thin I've become? Like a model! Ha! I'm so light I flew out of their hands and landed on my head."

"I am so sorry."

She patted my head and smoothed my hair with one wrinkled hand. "I've got no one but you."

"Are you in pain?"

"They feed me pills. To knock me out. I wait until they turn around and spit them out."

"What can I do?"

"Go to Rome."

"I'm afraid for you."

"Leave me here with the beast. Did she take everything like I said she would? *Eine bestia.*"

"Yes."

"And your father the idiot? Where is he?"

"On his way to Australia."

"Oy. Such a *shlimaazel*, and spending your money."

"There's nothing I can do."

"I'm tired...I want to sleep."

"I love you, Grandma."

"Paint beautiful pictures for me?"

"Yes."

She closed her eyes and turned her bandaged head to the wall. I sat for a time, I couldn't tell how long, and wept. She was ninety-six years old. Small, pale and wrinkled, with skin like the finest, most transparent parchment.

The halls were starting to rustle with activity. Nurses were waking patients with thermometers and breakfast and their first medication of the day.

I stood up and kissed the top of my grandmother's head. The hair was fine and silver gray, her head was warm and dry. Then I walked quietly out of the room, stopping at the desk to make sure that the nurse that had dropped her would never touch her again.

Chapter 32

Diary Entry

NYC
February 26, 1974

Today was our final session. Everything was the same as it had always been. The chairs were in their proper place; the sandbox stood in the corner, toy soldiers planted in strategic battle positions. I couldn't imagine what must have been going on in the session prior to mine.

Roberta seemed a bit preoccupied, unusually scattered. I feared I was already a part of the past. We got down to business rather quickly.

"There are some papers you need to sign today."

"I know."

"How do you feel?"

"Nervous."

"You'll continue on the medication until you feel like you'd like to stop?"

"How will I know when it's time?"

"You'll know. Here's the name of a therapist in Rome, in case something comes up, and you know you may call me anytime. We will continue to check in by phone once a week."

"I'd like that."

"I just want to say how proud I am of you."

"For what?"

"For coming through this as well as you have."

"I owe you my life."

We eyed each other, not knowing quite how to proceed. Roberta took a document out of a file and placed it on her desk.

"Why don't you come over here and take a look at the document."

She pulled a chair next to her desk and signaled for me to sit down.

I read over the document slowly. My hand shook as I signed, little beads of sweat forming behind my knees.

"It's official! You're a free woman!"

We stood up in unison and threw our arms around each other.

"Why do I feel so incredibly sad?"

"We will stay in close touch. OK? I am here if you need me. And I will miss you."

"I've never known anyone who was so kind."

"You deserve kindness. Try to believe that. The world is full of good people."

"I'm afraid."

"I have total trust that you'll be fine."

"I don't know what to say."

"I've had Ella prepare a special dinner and Dr. Blau

and his daughter are going to stop by for dessert. Then tomorrow, I've arranged for a car to take you to the airport. Am I correct, your flight is at six p.m.?"

"Yes."

"Congratulations! I've got one last patient and then we'll celebrate!"

I walked down the hallway to my room. *My room.* And I felt elated. I was starting out on my path, my life. I felt terrified, and excited, sad, and elated. So many emotions all at once, I thought my heart would burst.

Later that evening, we dined in the main dining room instead of the kitchen. The silver candelabra was lit, and Ella had set the table with the therapist's best china and silver. It was like the holiday of my dreams, but Bonsha Schweig was not the caterer. Ella prepared a fine meal of beautifully seasoned London broil and baked potatoes with sour cream, followed by a green salad with a French tarragon vinaigrette and a slice of Stilton cheese accompanied by a freshly baked baguette and Danish butter.

Dr. Blau and Annie appeared just as the chocolate Sacher torte was being brought to the table. There was schlag for the torte and strong coffee, and at the very end, a bottle of champagne was opened, and we drank a toast to my trip to Rome and then Ella sang her favorite hymn.

I was filled with gratitude. To have this family materialize just at this moment seemed to havebeen divine intervention.

Letter to Lizzie

NYC
February 28, 1974
10pm, aboard Alitalia Airlines Flight 40023 to Rome

My Dearest Lizzie,

Thank you for your last letter. What a fine joke that ridiculous letter from your lover, Transylvanian Count Igor. You're in fine form and up to your old tricks! I know you are still alive because the letter was written in your own handwriting!! HA! I will admit, after I had a good laugh, I did use it to prove my case. It showed that I had "killed" you! And those newspaper articles! In Italian! What genius! I'm on my way to Rome, am sending this letter special delivery and hope that you and Igor will be there greet me! The only thing that might keep you away would be other artistic commitments or a change of residence. In which case, you must leave word where you can be found at your old place.

With much love in my heart,

Ta Bête,

XOXOXOXOXOXO
Bette

THE END